'Not your typical book on dr[...] because it's mysterious, but [...] like an ancient and beautifu[...] written in two time periods; you can see how the past evolves into the present.'

(James, aged 12)

'The Maydew Witch is a good witch, and Gregor is great. I also like the funny bits, like when Suzie sticks her bottom in the window.'

(Rosie, aged 7)

'My favourite character is Gregor, the sheepdog, he is very naughty, and I like the suspense near the end when Isabel travels back in time to help Sally, as I didn't know what was going to happen to her.'

(Jasmine, aged 11)

'I would love to meet the sea dragon.'

(Jade, aged 11)

Look out for more of

THE PORTLAND CHRONICLES

The Enchantment of the Black Dog

The Portland Pirates

The Island Giant

Visit www.rovingpress.co.uk

THE PORTLAND CHRONICLES

THE
PORTLAND
SEA DRAGON

CAROL HUNT

ROVING PRESS

© 2010 Carol Hunt
Published by Roving Press Ltd
4 Southover Cottages, Frampton, Dorset, DT2 9NQ, UK
Tel: +44 (0)1300 321531
www.rovingpress.co.uk

This is a work of fiction. The characters, incidents and dialogues
are products of the author's imagination and are not to be
construed as real. Any resemblance to actual events or persons,
living or dead, is entirely coincidental.

First published 2010 by Roving Press Ltd
ISBN: 978-1-906651-05-3

British Library Cataloguing in Publication Data
A catalogue record for this book is available from the British
Library

Illustrations and cover artwork by Domini Deane

Set in Minion 11.5/14 pt by www.beamreachuk.co.uk
Printed and bound by Polska Books

PORTLAND
A MYSTERIOUS PLACE

Hi, my name's Isabel Maydew, I'm 12 years old and I live on the Isle of Portland in the south of England, an amazing, rocky place. I live with my mum, who sings, and sister Suzie, who's four-and-a-half, in a small house in Westcliff overlooking the sea. Hundreds of shipwrecks lie just below the cliffs where we live, in an area called Deadman's Bay.

Portland is well known for its history, and its fantastic animals, which sort of explains my favourite book. It's called *Monsteres of the Air and Sea* and it describes all the different kinds of dragon that used to live here. It has belonged to the Maydew family for generations, and I always felt it was destined to be mine. Don't be surprised about the dragons – they used to be quite common. Even today you can find fossilised ammonites in the rocks around Portland, like giant prehistoric snails, and dinosaur footprints in the stone quarries.

There are lots of stories on Portland about smugglers and mermaids, all of them true. This is my own story, about the Portland sea dragon, and it begins at midnight, 31 December 2010.

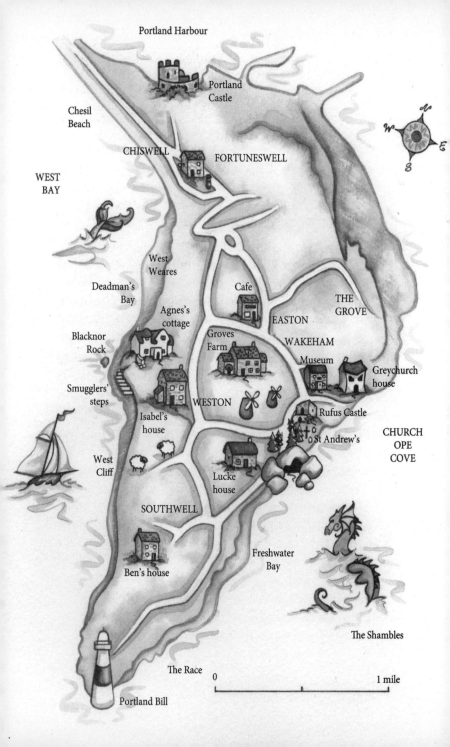

CHAPTER ONE

NEW YEAR'S EVE 2010

THE SEA DRAGON APPEARS

Isabel fell out of the bedroom window of the Portland cottage where she lived and dangled limply by one leg, her foot caught up in the curtain. 'Oh no,' she cried. The heavy green and gold book under her arm had unbalanced her as she had tried to climb quietly out of the window, and now she was stuck. She shuffled a bit, swaying backwards and forwards.

'Isabel, are you out of the window again?' yelled her mother up the stairs. 'We're about to sing *Auld Lang Syne* – it's nearly midnight. Come on, it *is* New Year's Eve! Hurry up.'

'Oh no,' muttered Isabel again. 'I'm *not* singing, no way.'

She twisted around so she was now dangling by one arm and one leg, gripping the windowsill, and started to pull herself back up. She peered into the bedroom. Her sister Suzie was right in front of her, stuffed sheep gripped under one arm, staring at her accusingly. 'You said you'd take me next time,' she said.

'Yes, I did,' said Isabel, dragging herself back into the room, 'and I will, when you're bigger, ok? You can't reach the kitchen roof at the moment. Your legs are too short.'

1

'Well, at least I don't hang around upside down with my bottom showing,' sneered Suzie. 'Why did you have that dragon book out there anyway?'

'It's called *Monsteres of the Air and Sea* and it's a very important Maydew family heirloom.'

Suzie snorted as Isabel thrust the large tatty book at her. 'Hold it for a minute while I take my shoes off. Look at the first page. "*This Booke belongs to Agnes Maydew, Born in the Year of Our Lord 1590.*" Isn't that amazing? Our own ancestor!'

'What does the bit underneath say?' asked Suzie.

'Isn't it time you learned to read? It says "*Sally Lucke*".'

'No, the bit about the dragon. I don't do reading at nursery school. I do Movement to Music and a little bit of drawing.'

'Well, fair enough,' admitted Isabel, 'It says, "*Sally Lucke, Taken by the Sea Dragon on a Tragick Nighte, January 1616*".'

'Wow,' said Suzie. 'Perhaps he'll pop back later and take you. I could write in the book, "*Isabel Maydew, Tooken by the Sea Dragon on a Happy Night, Love Suzie*".'

'If you could write …'

Suzie glared at her.

'I know,' said Isabel, 'Movement to Music, blah blah.'

They could hear their mother singing downstairs in a warbling high voice, with the television turned up full blast. Suzie had a knowing look on her face. 'You were going to look for the sea dragon again, weren't you?'

Isabel shrugged. 'It had crossed my mind,' she said casually.

'Your hair is all spiked up …'

Isabel looked in the mirror. Her light brown hair stood out around her face like a dandelion clock. Her grey eyes were wild and sparkling.

'… Like a hedgehog.' Suzie prodded her finger at the book. 'Read it to me,' she ordered.

Isabel sighed and read: "*Beware, for the Southern Sea Dragon is a fearful beast. During the earliest tymes, there were over twenty kyndes of Sea Dragon roaming the southern seas of Englande, the temperate Climate being suited to these Creatures. In these tymes, but one or two Species remain.*"

She gazed out of the window. 'Sometimes, I feel it's out there, looking for me.'

'Mum told me a story about the Maydew witch, who rescued a sea dragon hundreds of years ago. The dragon was hurt and she saved it,' said Suzie.

Isabel felt the familiar flip of butterflies in her stomach. She was desperate to learn more about her ancestor the Maydew witch and the sea dragon. Isabel felt certain that she, and she alone, would discover the truth about the dragon and what had really happened to Sally Lucke on that Tragick Nighte in January 1616.

Later, she thought, pushing Suzie towards the spiral staircase at the edge of her room. 'We'd better go down and sing or we'll never hear the end of it.'

An arrow-shot east across the island from Isabel's home was a freshly painted white house overlooking the narrow road leading to Rufus Castle. There, Mrs Greychurch, an old friend of Isabel's family, dreamt of swords and serpents with long jagged tails, as she spluttered loudly between snores.

'Take that, you beast,' she bellowed, as she tackled the evil dragon, waking herself up with a start. 'What's that?' She looked around the bedroom nervously.

Mrs Greychurch was superstitious about New Year's Eve, especially the horrible moment at midnight when the old year finally gave way to the new. She peered at the red numbers of her alarm clock, blinking a steady 12:00 at her. She shuddered. She hated midnight. The darkness threatened to stretch out forever, swallowing her up, like a huge dragon.

A crash downstairs jolted her fully awake. She jumped out of bed and wrapped a frilly orange dressing gown over her nightdress. Clutching the broom she kept by the bed, she tiptoed down the stairs. The door to the dining room was open, and an icy chill wafted through the house from an open window.

'Who's there?' she called, 'I'm armed!'

The draught from the wide-open French window blew her papers across the floor and there was a loud flapping noise like a huge bird. Mrs Greychurch clutched the broom to her chest, her eyes wide with terror. There, in the dark garden, something gazed back at her with clear yellow eyes.

Petrified with fear, she gasped, 'A dragon, I knew it. After all these years! I knew that one day I would see the evil creature for myself!'

She pulled herself together and advanced into the garden brandishing the broom. The dragon spread its mighty wings and leaped in a swirling motion into the air, leaving a whirlwind in its wake which dragged Mrs Greychurch's gown virtually over her head.

'I can see you, you hideous monster. Oh yes, I can,' she screamed from under the orange frills. 'You will pay for your crimes against my family, against our dear Sally. Murderous beast! I know you killed her!'

Slamming the window and staggering indoors, she fell on the sofa, sobbing. She had always believed in dragons. In fact, she was convinced that she, Veronica Greychurch, would one day avenge her ancestor's terrible murder.

She sat up and rebuttoned her gown with trembling fingers. She must get a grip on herself. Her daughter Miranda, home from boarding school for the holidays, must be protected from this curse, which had hung over her family for generations. Her own grandmother, in every other way as mad as a box of frogs, had always said that one day the dragon would return. And now she was right.

She went over to the dark wooden desk in the corner of the room and rifled through her bookcase. She had recently researched a booklet for the Portland Museum about Sally Lucke and her mysterious disappearance on the night of the terrible storm of 4 January 1616. Finding the story, she read it aloud in a dramatic voice, just as her grandmother had read it to her, although her eyes were not as twitchy as her grandmother's.

"*There were great waves rolling black in the darke night and the villagers took shelter in their homes,*" she exclaimed.

"*There were rains of hail that drummed the roofs and caused much fear among the good people of the Island. For certain the sins of the ungodly were being visited upon us all. There were those who ventured forth in this dismal weather to attend to their animals, God's poor creatures, which cannot hide from such storms. Whilst attending his flock, old John Muddle saw a terrible thinge in the skye,*" Mrs Greychurch pointed wildly at the ceiling.

"*A great beast that did swoop round and round as if in search of its prey. On this night, Sally Lucke was lost. A beauty she was, who met a cursed end, devoured by the strange serpent of the skye.*"

Mrs Greychurch glanced up at a portrait on the wall. The small oval painting showed a fair young woman, who would have been very beautiful if her eyes had not been quite so close together or her smile quite so smug. Mrs Greychurch was distantly related to Sally through Sally's younger brother, Richard Lucke, a quarryman. Her story had been passed down in the family since her disappearance on the night of the 1616 storm. Mrs Greychurch sighed as she thought about poor Sally. She had always dreamed of solving the mystery of her tragic end.

'Tonight', she announced, 'At the start of my fifty-first year, I now have proof that the evil dragon lives on! Perhaps he is seeking out his next prey, some poor unsuspecting woman …'

She clutched her nightgown to her neck and shivered. No doubt he had been drawn to her, both by her beauty (she shook her tangled hair out of her face) and by her family connection to Sally.

Rising proudly to her feet, her chin jutting forward, the broom clasped like a spear by her side, she looked out at the eerie moonlit night. 'Well, he has met his match,' she cried aloud. She would find the dragon and kill it, once and for all. It was her destiny.

Agnes Maydew was walking peacefully by the cliffs at Blacknor Point, along the west coast of the island. It was hard to believe it was New Year's Day, so mild and warm it was. A light misty rain fell around her and sparkled in her soft brown hair. It had been a long night and she had slept badly, as she often did at the turn of the year. A hazardous time, she always felt, when doors opened between the past and the future.

Far below her a movement in the sea caught her eye. Ripping across the surface, dipping in and out of the water, was a strange creature. With a long jagged tail and huge green and gold wings as wide as Agnes's cottage, it was an extraordinary animal, a sea dragon. Dragons were so rare that Agnes was stunned. She gasped and put her hand over her mouth, hardly able to believe her eyes. The dragon moved gracefully, with a lightness that was amazing for its size. Agnes thought of her precious book *Monsteres of the Air and Sea*. She had often gazed at pictures of these animals, but never thought she would see one herself.

As the dragon spun across the sea, he hooked a claw through a fishing net, which twisted and tightened around his leg. The animal seemed confused and in pain as he dragged himself out of the water to the rocks at the foot of the cliffs. He limped to a halt, his eyes closed tightly against the agony in his leg.

Agnes knew at once she must help the dragon. The islanders often brought their animals to her for healing, and she was not afraid of any animal, even one as rare and unusual as a dragon. She ran down the white steps cut into the rock, leading to the foot of the West Cliff. Walking carefully towards the sea dragon, she exclaimed, 'I see you are hurt. Do not be alarmed, *I* will not hurt you.'

As she approached, the dragon looked helplessly at the small young woman in front of him. She had steady grey eyes and long brown hair in a plait down her back. Her gentle hands tugged and pulled at the net still tangled around his leg, undoing it as quickly as possible. He looked at her with large round eyes and went to snap at her. She smacked him on the nose and he blinked in shock.

'Naughty dragon – that's no way to thank me! There, the net is now off. But wait for me a moment.' She quickly ran back up the cliff steps, across the grassy field to a cottage a short distance from the cliffs and disappeared inside, reappearing with a small earthenware pot. Returning to the dragon, she zigzagged briskly down the limestone cliff steps, then took his leg in her small hands.

'I use this ointment for wounds, it will help you.' Her movements were reassuring and certain as she applied the mixture. The dragon licked her gratefully. 'There, that is the best I can do for you. Now be gone.'

The dragon slowly got to his feet. Then, with a thankful backward glance, he flapped his great wings and took off.

Agnes watched till he dipped below the waves. Then she took a winding path at the foot of the cliffs, visible only at low tide, leading north around the island to the edge of Deadman's Bay, where many shipwrecks lay beneath the water. She was as sure-footed as a mountain goat, having walked this way many times. Today the sea was a deceptively serene blue. To the north, Chesil Beach twisted along the coast under a glistening sea mist. Agnes clambered across the jutting rocks until she came to dark Blacknor Rock. She stood there, her hands on her hips, waiting, aware of eyes watching her from the sea.

'Ssister, you called me?'

Agnes jumped as a mermaid suddenly appeared as if from nowhere. With her long red-gold hair curling around her, the mermaid flipped her turquoise tail and slid on to a rock above the surface of the sea, a short distance from her. Agnes watched her warily. The sea people were enchanting, charming and clever. The mermaid smiled back at her with glowing green eyes.

Agnes, her voice ringing clearly across the waves, spoke first. 'The sea dragon is awake, mermaid. He's an old creature, belonging to ancient times when there were fewer people to fear him. He's not awoken before in my lifetime. What d' you know of this?'

'Who knowss why a ssea dragon should awaken,' hissed the mermaid, shrugging her white shoulders. 'Why should I care? Sso, perhaps a few people will be eaten. Since when does the Maydew witch deal with ssuch matters as a ssea dragon? She iss too grand for uss sea creatures … Sshall I kill it for you? Iss that what you wish?'

'No, you know that's not right,' Agnes almost spat the

10

words at the mermaid. 'The sea dragon has no idea of people and they no idea of it. What more d' you know? Why is he awake? Why now? You're not being straight with me, fish girl.'

She glared at the mermaid, who curled her lip, showing sharp teeth.

'You're too susspicious, ssister. The ssea dragon wakess when he iss called. I know no more,' said the mermaid and with a smug flick of her tail, she was gone. Agnes shivered uneasily. She planned to return to the cottage and consult her book *Monsteres of the Air and Sea*. A sea dragon was a bad omen.

Isabel walked along the main road through the village of Weston, towards Southwell, past the fields to one side and quiet houses to the other, gripping Suzie's mittened hand. It was a sluggish time of year when no one except them ever seemed to be out. Boring and quiet. The sun was already sliding low in the yellowish sky. Suzie wore a pink tutu over her red wellington boots, and orange tights. Isabel tried not to look at her. The fake tiger fur coat on top looked quite ridiculous and was the last embarrassing straw. She sighed.

Suddenly a shadow flashed over them and, as Isabel gazed up, her heart beating faster with excitement, she felt the whoomph of great wings beating in the sky. In a second, it vanished as suddenly as it had appeared.

'Did you see that?' she cried.

'What, the big bird?' said Suzie, uninterested. 'Not really. I want to see the Portland sheep. Not some smelly old bird. D' you know, I'm making signs for the supermarket. They sell dead lambs. It's horrible. They put bits of them in the meat aisle.' She gazed up at Isabel with large, sincere blue eyes.

Isabel sighed again. 'I'm sure it was a dragon. I wonder if Ben saw it.'

' 'Spect so,' said Suzie. 'Mum says you are both at a funny age and we should be kind to you.' Suzie patted her arm.

They paused at the field where the island sheep were grazing on the stubby winter grass and Suzie climbed on to the gate. The cold wind blew steadily across the field towards them, hardly ruffling the sturdy sheep with their curling horns. Suzie gazed at them lovingly.

'Can I take one home? I'll put it in the garden and it can eat grass,' said Suzie. 'Mum wouldn't need to mow the lawn.'

'Yes, whatever,' said Isabel absent-mindedly, still thinking about the sea dragon.

'Great!' said Suzie. 'We can grab one. I'll stuff it up my jumper.' She looked up and down the empty road, theatrically. 'No one will ever know,' she whispered loudly.

'They will,' said Isabel. 'We found out what happened to your pet guinea pig, remember?'

Suzie shrugged coolly. 'He looked better with hair spray. Anyway I only did the bit between his ears. It went spiky and he loved it. He wanted to look cool in case he met a lady guinea pig.'

In the distance, a figure emerged from one of the Southwell houses that overlooked the western fields of the island. It was Ben Lau, their friend, who had known Isabel since an incident at Bumbletots nursery school many years ago, when Isabel had eaten the fleece lining of her new winter coat and been violently sick over Ben. Now, aged twelve, he and Isabel were exactly the same height, liked the same music and disagreed about everything else. He wandered towards them. He was wrapped in hat, scarf and gloves and over the top a large black coat. A few spikes of black hair covered one of his dark brown eyes.

'Did you see Isabel's dragon?' asked Suzie.

'I can see very little,' he said coolly, 'Unless I move my fringe like this. Now I can see anything at a 45 degree angle from my face. Izzie's probably been driven mad by your mother's singing, as I suspect from reading her text messages about dragons. If she's seen something, I would say it's most likely to be a type of pliosaur.'

'Dragon,' hissed Isabel. 'A southern sea dragon.'

'If you insist,' said Ben, looking at her with one narrowed eye. 'But technically a pliosaur. Or it could just be an imaginary friend.'

'I wonder if it's hungry,' said Suzie.

Ben removed a glove and fished a half-eaten piece of Christmas cake in kitchen roll out of his pocket. 'Pretty starving if it hasn't eaten since the Jurassic period,' he said. 'I expect it would target some dumb animal like a sheep.'

'If he did eat a dumb animal, he'd eat you first,' said Suzie, looking at the cake in Ben's hand. 'You're fat enough.'

Ben looked at Suzie with a one eyed sneer. 'I think you'll find there are two reasons why dinosaurs died out. Number one, they were stupid and, number two, they tasted good, so mammals ate them.'

'Everyone knows that a meteor killed them,' argued Suzie.

Isabel was walking a couple of paces ahead of them, her eyes fixed nervously on the looming Greychurch house. It was spooky, like Mrs Greychurch. The windows were wide and black like empty eye sockets, the door a gaping skull's mouth. Isabel half-expected to see teeth around the door frame.

She took the front steps slowly. She wobbled on the top step, reached for the doorknocker and found herself grasping thin air. A cold-eyed Mrs Greychurch stood in front of her, looking her up and down.

'Ah, Isabel,' she said at last, and sniffed as if a dead fish had flopped on the doorstep.

She peered past the trembling girl, up and down the road, then sneakily up at the sky, as though looking for something. Finally, pursing her orange lipsticked lips, she pulled herself up to her full height and glared at Isabel. She was scary, with her white hair scraped back off her face and a strange blonde hairpiece attached at the back.

'Mrs Groves at the farm wanted me to collect some biscuits for Gregor,' ventured Isabel.

'Ah yes, bless him, the poor dog, he loves my biscuits. Come in quickly, it's cold and there may be something out there,' said Mrs Greychurch. She slammed the door behind Isabel and pressed her back against it.

'But Ben and Suzie are out there,' exclaimed Isabel. Mrs Greychurch's stare made her uneasy. Her arms were covered in goose bumps and she was trying not to shiver.

'Have you managed to ride a horse yet?' said Mrs Greychurch, changing the subject. 'Of course, my daughter Miranda is of professional standard,' she added coolly.

'I have been riding, yes …'

'It's all about control. Keep the reins tight, get a firm grip on the animal. Don't let him sense your fear.'

Mrs Greychurch stared fiercely into Isabel's eyes. 'Tell me, and don't lie. Have you seen anything unusual, perhaps something large, flying around the island?'

Isabel tried to take a step backwards. 'No, Mrs Greychurch,' she said, keeping eye contact.

Mrs Greychurch hissed between her teeth. Neither she nor Isabel blinked. 'If there is something out there, I can tell you, it won't get the better of me. I know people are hiding it. Secrets! There are people with secrets on this island. But a Greychurch will not stand for them. I will winkle them out, find them, and put a stop to them!'

Isabel froze against the door.

'I trust your mother's well?' Mrs Greychurch said finally. 'The church choir depends on her marvellous singing voice.' She picked up a box of biscuits from the hall table. Isabel seized the moment to fling open the door, mumbling a hasty 'Thank you'. She dashed with relief, clutching the box, into the bright winter air, her boots clumping down the steps. Mrs Greychurch peered around the door at the sky with strange wide eyes.

Almost colliding with Ben and Suzie, Isabel panted, 'Can you take Suzie home for me? There's something weird going on. I just have to run by Groves Farm with these biscuits for Gregor and pick up my fleece.' Isabel was a disastrous horse rider and her jacket had been trashed in a fall.

'Weird, eh?' said Ben. He and Suzie smirked at one another.

'Don't let Suzie steal sheep, it's illegal and everyone will blame me,' Isabel called after them as she rushed off.

Ben shrugged his shoulders as they plodded back up the road. 'Doesn't bother me,' he said.

Suzie smiled hopefully.

CHAPTER FOUR

NEW YEAR'S DAY 1616

THE INFAMOUS SALLY LUCKE

On the low stone wall that surrounded the small garden beside Agnes's thatched cottage, on the far edge of the small island village of Weston, Sally Lucke sat in the sunshine, kicking her legs, waiting for Agnes to return. The sun glinted on her white-gold hair and her sharp blue eyes. She liked to spy on Agnes from time to time, it was always useful. Today had offered her a mine of fascinating information. She had found Agnes's book lying on the table, a grand green and gold affair with pictures of strange creatures, and dragons. Sally had wondered whether such fantastic creatures as dragons could still exist, as she leafed through the pages.

'I would see one of those weird creatures. It would be fine to have a dragon do my bidding,' she mused aloud. 'I would call a dragon from beneath the sea to aid me at my will. It may even be valuable. Indeed I surely could make the beast act for me and bring terror to the stupid islanders.'

Sally smiled gleefully to herself, sliding the book under her long shawl. She would borrow the book. Agnes, with all her learning, would not mind at all.

As for the mermaid, Sally had stood at the top of the

cliffs watching Agnes talking with the creature. What a vile, slimy thing that was. Sally shuddered. Agnes dabbled in some strange areas. No wonder the locals called her a witch.

'How horrible to live always under the sea with a tail and never walk on warm ground. That's the worst fate I can imagine,' she mused. 'Mermaids are such unnatural creatures.'

As Agnes returned to the cottage, Sally hopped down to pretend she had just arrived. 'Cousin, how are you today?' she called cheerfully, entering the dark cottage after her. Agnes was replacing a bottle of potion inside the coolness of the chimney.

'I'm well. What brings you? Is your mother better?'

'She would improve at once if my father drank less,' said Sally.

'She has all the children to care for too, could you not help her more?' asked Agnes. Sally shrugged. They had talked about this many times. 'I have my sights set on bigger things,' she said, smiling to herself. Agnes looked at her seriously. 'Joseph Groves plays a fast game with young women, Sally, beware. His promises are worth nothing.'

Sally held up her hand and waved her slender fingers at Agnes. 'He'll give me a ring. Never have I had eyes for any other. Indeed, when we were children, he always said one day we should be wed. He said I am the most beautiful girl on the island.'

'Don't believe what he tells you,' said Agnes sharply. 'Where d' you imagine the islanders find their tobacco and brandy? He's no simple lad, these days. He's a smuggler, that's how he paid for his fine horse and velvet coat. He'll set harsh terms for a ring, be sure of it. He casts his eye over a different girl every Sunday at chapel, as you well know. He has high views of himself. He'll not marry beneath him.'

Sally clenched her fists. 'I expect you want me to live the life of my mother, stuck with an old drunk and more children than she needs. I'll have a grand life over at Groves Farm, and then you will envy me! The islanders will curtsey and doff their hats to *me*.'

Agnes reached up to grasp her taller cousin's shoulders. 'Take care, Sally, I feel there is much afoot in your mind and it takes dangerous paths. Your father loves you and your mother does her best. It's a good ambition to do better, but you will go too far one day. Across the country, witches hang by the neck for their good efforts. Plagues and fires are laid at our door. Joseph Groves will play fast and loose. You'll not tame him. Why not come live with me here, for now, and help tend the gardens?'

Sally laughed and grabbed her cousin's rough hands. 'And end with hands like these? Who would look at me then? You can keep your gardens.'

As Sally opened the door, she turned back to Agnes. 'You would do well, Cousin, to consider how much better it will be for *you* when I marry Joseph Groves. You're alone here now, too young to be widowed and scraping by with your vegetables and herbs. You have a young daughter to raise on your own. I could bring you much better things, a chance to mix with higher folk.'

Sally looked with disgust around the simple room and left, slamming the door behind her.

Agnes sat alone by the kitchen table. It was a good thing Sally had not arrived earlier to see the sea dragon at the foot of the cliffs. Agnes looked around the room with a slight frown. Surely she had left her book *Monsteres of the Air and Sea* on the kitchen table? Could Sally have taken the book with her?

Agnes shook her head with concern. Ancient creatures like dragons were difficult to deal with in the modern world of the 1600s, she mused. People were fearful of such things nowadays and would kill a dragon as soon as look at it. Dragons and people could not live together easily. She must find a way to deal with it, for its own sake, so that it would leave the islanders alone, so that it would be safe.

Agnes made a huffing sound as she rose to her feet. It would be difficult. In these times, people no longer respected her and the old ways. The islanders called her a witch, with her garden of herbs and rare flowers. Agnes wondered what would happen to them all, fearing for the dragon and for herself. 'Dragons bring a time of terrible change,' she thought. 'I am not sure we are ready for this here on the island.'

Isabel walked slowly along the track that led to Groves Farm. She kept one eye on the sky, which made walking difficult. Mrs Greychurch must have seen something too. The sea dragon was nearby, she was sure of it.

'I just want to see it,' she said quietly.

Groves Farm was slap bang in the middle of the island, and had been there, virtually unchanged, since the Middle Ages. Isabel passed strips of field separated by mounds of earth and crumbled old stone walls, held together by wire. Some of the larger fields had held flocks of island sheep, but now only one flock remained in a far flung field to the west. There was an air of disrepair about the farm, run by her mother's cousin, Mrs Groves.

The fields close to the farmhouse now contained various horses, peacefully grazing the sparse grass. Many of the horses were old and retired from duties. Some were related to the big old island horses that worked in the stone quarries.

A frantic baying noise came from the farmhouse and Gregor, the farm sheepdog, hurtled around the corner, slipping on the wet ground, then accelerating at her. He skidded into her legs and sank his teeth into her trousers, tugging at her wildly, his black and white collie tail waving like a flag.

'No, Gregor, don't. Get off!' she cried as she fell backwards on to the muddy yard, the biscuits crashing from the box into the mud.

A willowy girl with a mane of fine blonde hair drifted across the yard. It was Miranda, Mrs Greychurch's only daughter, now living away from home during term time at a boarding school near Sherborne. Although she was a year older than Isabel, like Ben she had known Isabel since nursery school. Miranda had always been very popular and for some reason saw Isabel as her sworn enemy. They had sometimes played together in the sand box but Miranda always poured water over Isabel's castles.

'Gregor, come,' she said. Immediately Gregor let go of Isabel and gazed like an angel at the girl, as she leaned over to pat him.

'Silly girl,' she said to Isabel. "Course he's going to bite you if you lie down.'

'He bites everyone!' snapped Isabel.

'No, only the village idiot,' smirked Miranda, in clean jodhpurs and a snowy white shirt. She swept by Isabel, looking down at Isabel's muddy trousers.

Isabel made a gesture at Miranda's back and felt better. Gregor chomped happily through the biscuits on the ground, making loud crunching noises.

Isaac whinnied loudly behind her and Isabel jumped. He was a large brown horse with a white stripe down his nose. Chewing glumly on bits of dry hay, he watched out of the corner of his eye as she walked towards him. Isabel reached as far into her pocket as she could. There were a couple of old mints there. She dangled her hand over the stable door and Isaac shifted happily. He ate the mints gratefully, showing big teeth like a row of dirty tombstones.

'It's your fault about the fleece. Why do you have to throw me all the time?' Isaac curled his lip as though he was smiling.

Isabel gazed up at the farmhouse at the end of the stable yard. It looked like it had been constructed in bits and pieces. It was a long building, in places only one room deep, with high crooked chimneys. Part of the house sagged lower than the rest, like an old barn. With few windows, it was always dark inside. A bit spooky, Isabel thought, as though the place was full of the ghosts of all the people who had lived there. In the dining room, her favourite room in the house, were grand portraits of Groves ancestors.

Isabel found Mrs Groves among them, standing thoughtfully in front of a large painting of a grey racehorse. Looking down at her were the huge paintings of imposing, handsome Joseph Groves holding a horse whip, fatherly, kind-eyed Peter Groves, untidy Robert Groves, and many more. The women appeared in smaller portraits and all looked like Mrs Groves. A mirror at the other end extended the room forever into a long, long table, with the Groves family stretching in an infinite line.

'Good grief, you scared me!' yelped Mrs Groves at Isabel. 'I was miles away, thinking about Harry, the racehorse.' She stepped hastily away from the painting and smoothed her fair wispy hair. Mrs Groves was dressed as always in trousers and a knitted dark green jumper, with crumbs embedded in the wool.

'Have you remembered about this evening?' she asked, abruptly. Isabel looked blank. Surely not another riding lesson?

'I will be on television this evening in *An Audience with Louisa Smith-Forsythe*,' she announced as she bustled into the kitchen. 'Where is that dog now? I cannot turn my back for five minutes. Did you let him out? He'll be out there messing around in the stable yard. He'll be filthy. Gregor, come here!' she bellowed from the kitchen door.

Gregor trotted in cheerfully, looking up at Mrs Groves expectantly, his fur soaked with wet mud, biscuits and slobber around his mouth.

'For goodness sake, look at the state of your paws. I could cry, honestly I could. I do wish people would show more consideration. Don't I have enough to do without all this? I never get time to sit down. He's in, then he's out …'

She scooped up a carrier bag with a soggy fleece inside and thrust it at Isabel without looking at her.

Conjuring up a biscuit for Gregor, she sighed, 'Here you are then. Don't crunch it over the carpet. Oh no, I just hoovered in here. Look at the mess. No, sit there, don't move until I get your blanket.' Gregor continued to crunch, crumbs flying. Mrs Groves sighed again.

'Yes, Louisa Smith-Forsythe, the famous TV psychic. It was filmed last night at the Pavilion in Weymouth. "Psychic Wows Weymouth", it said in the *Dorset Echo*.' She rustled the newspaper at Isabel.

'Oh yes. Of course,' Isabel said, glancing at her watch.

'It's getting a bit cold,' said Mrs Groves. 'Do you want me to call your mother to come and get you? Oh no, don't roll on the rug, you naughty dog!'

'I'll be fine,' said Isabel, thinking that it was warmer outdoors than in the old farmhouse. Gregor jumped up and sniffed heavily around her, hoping to find a dropped crumb. He gazed at her in obvious disappointment and growled.

'No, Gregor, she's got nothing for you. I'm afraid she forgot those nice biscuits from Mrs Greychurch, didn't she. But never mind, you're getting fat anyway,' Mrs Groves scolded as she ushered Isabel out of the door.

Isabel took the footpath that led towards the old windmills. It was four o'clock and a bright darkness, like the start of a solar eclipse, was drawing in. She paused, feeling odd, as if she had lost her balance for a moment, like standing on a seesaw. In the far distance she thought she heard wings flapping, and strange white lightning forked silently from the clouds to the ground over Portland Harbour. In the eerie light, a rainbow arced across the sky to the east of the island, from the Harbour to the Shambles, and glowed intensely for just a few seconds before fading into the grey clouds. Isabel headed east towards the rainbow, to the woods at Church Ope Cove. There, she ran through the tall trees, certain that the dragon must be nearby.

There were footsteps approaching and low voices, people talking quietly, furtively. Isabel stepped behind one of the old chestnut trees as a dark angry man strode past, twigs crackling under his feet.

CHAPTER SIX

NEW YEAR'S DAY 1616

SMUGGLERS RIDE OUT

As darkness fell, the men slipped away from their island homes in Southwell and Weston. A thin slither of moon lit the way. They took overgrown paths, setting out for Church Ope Cove, greeting each other with slight nods. Two of them led horses, patiently clip-clopping along the footways as Joseph led the way, confident of his route despite the darkness. The moon slid behind clouds and the winter darkness had a velvety touch. As they took the path through the wood down to the cove, Joseph listened to the hushing sound of waves curling over the pebbles below.

'Least there's lanterns down there, it's black as a devil's glove up here, I can scarcely see my feet.'

Joseph and his men made their way through the overhanging oak trees, weaving down the steep, slippery path. As the ghostly shape of St Andrew's Church loomed ahead, they cut to the right and slid through brambles and bushes in a hidden route to the cove. They paused in the thin moonlight, letting their eyes adjust, before striding across the stones to the sea.

'Boats are in,' said one of Joseph's companions. 'A good haul of spirits, I hope.'

'Take the barrel,' called Joseph, as they reached the boats. 'It's too heavy for one man.'

There was laughter around him. 'He will have the silks and finery for his young wench, Sally Lucke, I expect. Truly he is bewitched.'

Joseph remained silent. The men pulled the boats farther up the shore, hats pulled low to conceal their faces and protect against the sharp sea breeze.

'Are you not afeared of her, Joseph lad? She would have you betrothed and at her beck and call. What if her cousin Agnes puts the evil eye on you?'

'Mind you, Sally is a fine looking girl,' one of them called over. 'We hear of her practising witchcraft in yon cottage with Agnes. Perhaps they will both enchant you into wedlock.'

'There is much to be done tonight,' said Joseph grimly. He turned to the dark figure beside him. 'Take the lantern. We must work well to get the haul up to the horses and away. The wind changes direction and the ship must sail. I fear we may be overlooked easy with all this light and noise.'

The men worked in silence, struggling back up the narrow path to the woods with the barrels and reams of silk and velvet. The boats heaved off with a quiet slap of the oars, heading for the gloomy ship beyond the cove.

Joseph stood for a moment alone, surveying the sea with satisfaction. This was a good haul and all had gone well. The farm struggled these days, the farm wealth of previous years dwindling, but smuggling meant that he could live as he pleased. Of course, there was a risk involved. Joseph smiled grimly to himself. He thought of the men working for him. Any one of them could betray him.

But the men were superstitious, like all the islanders, fearful of shadows and witches. It was no bad thing to be seen speaking to widow Agnes Maydew and young Sally Lucke. It was no bad thing for the men to fear him, too.

Joseph wondered if Agnes understood the risks she took, practising magic and healing arts. Times were changing and there was a different mood in the country under King James. There had been stories of the Witch Finder General from the mainland. Agnes would have to keep her wits about her, or find herself dunked in Weston pond, thought Joseph with a smirk.

As he turned to leave the beach, a splash behind him made him look sharply over his shoulder. He dropped to one knee and squinted into the hazy darkness. He could make out a shape looming up from the sea against the blackness of the waves, a curving snake-like shape, like smoke rising from the ashes of a fire.

Joseph hesitated, his eyes narrowed. The boats would have reached the ship by now. Whatever monster loomed from the deeps was no concern of his. There were shouts from the woods above.

'I have no time for sea monsters,' he muttered, running for the path, his hand instinctively grasping his sword.

The men held a struggling figure, his arm twisted behind his back.

'It's John Lucke. He saw us loading the cart.'

'No doubt you would like some lace for your daughter. I know that fair Sally would be easily pleased by such,' said Joseph, sheathing the sword in his belt. 'Give him some goods and send the old fool on his way.'

'Smugglers!' spat John Lucke, drunkenly. 'You should all hang. I know you, Joseph Groves. I know your voice. There is law now on this island and you cannot run your spoils through here. I will do God's work, I will denounce you!' The man's voice grew louder. At a gesture from Joseph, one of the men stuffed a cloth in his mouth.

'Tie him up, the old drunk,' commanded Joseph sharply, 'and throw him in the back of the cart. We ride to the cliffs at Deadman's Bay. Throw him over. The undertow will carry him away. No one will miss him.' The men dragged John Lucke away, his cries muffled and fading as they vanished into the woods.

Joseph stood still, waiting and listening. There had been the crack of a twig, the faintest sound, as if a watcher held their breath. Joseph knew that there was someone else present, someone watching and afraid.

He twirled his sword slowly between his fingers. He could not afford to miss a spy.

A small figure unfroze from the dark shadows beneath a tree. 'You're a murderer! Tell them to let him go!' the creature said, a child, strangely dressed in foreign garb.

Without hesitation, the only sound a hiss of metal, Joseph swung his sword through the air. There was a soft noise, like silk falling, and a flash of silvery light that zigzagged through the trees from the sky. The ghost vanished as mysteriously as she had appeared. Joseph prodded thoughtfully at the ground where she had been. He would remember that face and deal with her in due course. He strode purposefully after his men.

Isabel looked around her and shivered. She was alone again. The smuggler had gone, vanished into thin air. She could hardly believe what had just happened. She had travelled back to a time when smugglers roamed the island. Now she glimpsed the yellow street lights of Wakeham through the trees, and sighed with relief. She touched her finger lightly to her arm where a long thin gash was starting to darken with blood. The smuggler had not been a ghost – he had been as real as she was. The crisp northerly wind shook the bare branches of the trees above her, but a dim light came from the west. Hopefully, she could get home before it was completely dark.

Mrs Groves was clearly trying not to look at the camera as it whizzed above the audience, panning over her. She watched it from the corner of her eye like a nervous horse. She clutched her large black handbag in one hand and the picture of her beloved Harry in the other, a great racehorse in his day. Harry had died peacefully of old age some years ago, but Louisa Smith-Forsythe was famous for being able to contact animals on the 'other side'.

'Ladies and Gentlemen, the star of *Intimate Psychic Hour* and *Find That Ghost*, psychic medium Louisa Smith-Forsythe!' announced the voice-over. A hefty woman in a daringly low-cut peach dress with a long wrap around her shoulders took the stage.

'I am ready to get started right away,' she announced bossily, rubbing the palms of her hands together, her chest wobbling like two jellies. 'I will be making a connection today with many of our dear departed friends on the other side. I will bring through messages that prove beyond a shadow of a doubt the existence of life after death. I would like to join you all together tonight, bringing the two worlds very much closer. Now, I'm coming up here to the back,' she shouted, 'And, oh dear, I'm getting a father figure who passed on to the other side with a pain in the chest!'

She clutched her ample chest and looked anguished. Fifty hands shot up.

'Now I'm getting a B. B wants his family to know that he's all right now. Yes, love,' she added to an invisible person, apparently stood next to her. 'I'm telling them all about it.'

Louisa looked around the room. 'Do you know a Bert, lady at the back in the pink? Oh my, he says there is a terrible smell under the sink. Yes, my love, you need to get that pipe fixed.'

The lady in pink burst into tears. 'That's right. It must be my Bert. He was always concerned about the pipes under the sink.' The camera zoomed in on her for a close-up shot.

'He says he is with you still,' continued Louisa, 'But he doesn't like the new curtains. No, he doesn't. He says you wouldn't have bought them if he were still there.'

The lady sniffed loudly.

'He says he is glad he has proved to you today that there is life beyond the veil,' concluded Louisa triumphantly.

'But not curtains!' muttered Mrs Groves.

Louisa pursed her lips as she gazed around the room, finally pointing a trembling hand at Mrs Groves. She glowed with emotion and sweat. The TV camera rotated on its stand to focus on Mrs Groves.

'Now,' she paused for effect, 'I am getting a very powerful message. I am seeing an animal with a long nose.'

Mrs Groves gasped with delight.

'And wings, huge wings. Do you know of what I'm talking?'

Mrs Groves' face fell. She was sinking into her seat, as if she was trying to disappear.

'Now, come on, my love, this is a big animal. Oooh, how mysterious! Call me psychic, but I don't get messages like this every day. Do you know anything about this strange animal, my dear? Big creature, long nose, wings. If I weren't a down-to-earth lady, I would call this a dragon!'

The audience tittered. Mrs Grove shook her head again, unable to utter a word.

'We need some help with this message. In front of him I now see a tall dark gentleman, very handsome. He says his name is Joseph. He has an eye for the ladies. He says something about smuggling as well, I'm sure of that, what a dashing chap he is!' Louisa broke off to giggle, her large chest heaving.

'Oh, my goodness ...' Louisa dropped her voice to a dramatic hush. 'He says he got away with murder ... twice. He's holding up two fingers.' Around the room, there was an expectant silence.

'Ah,' said Mrs Groves, at last able to speak, 'Well, I've no idea, really. Could this animal be a horse?'

'No, dear. Too big,' said Louisa, 'Good heavens, I'm all flushed. They've faded now, my love.'

Mrs Groves was prodded by a young man with a clipboard and led away for her own piece to the camera, to be shown at the end of the programme.

'So, can you tell me ... um ... Mrs Groves, what animal you felt was being described by Louisa?'

'What animal?' said Mrs Groves in a high-pitched voice. 'Well, Harry was a big horse. He was fast in his day, a marvellous racehorse. He had an eye for the mares and lived to be a very old chap. I miss him terribly.' She dabbed her eyes vaguely with a bit of tissue. The clipboard man looked disappointed.

'No, I don't know anything about dragons or murderers. Oh, is that the time? Must dash. Gregor will be chewing the sofa and weeing on my best cushions,' she exclaimed, rushing for the exit.

Mrs Groves and Gregor hurried into the brightly lit cafe in Easton early in the morning to see Mrs Greychurch. They had been friends for many years. They settled in the garden for a long chat, Mrs Greychurch sipping a thin herbal tea and Mrs Groves with a large frothy coffee sprinkled with chocolate. Mrs Greychurch prodded one of the garden sculptures of a dragon with her umbrella, and Gregor sniffed around for a while, looking for lost cakes or biscuits. 'So I said, could it be Harry, my horse?' said Mrs Groves, while Mrs Greychurch stared past her, orange lips pursed. Mrs Greychurch was already bored. She would never hear the end of Mrs Groves' television adventure, she was sure. Gregor stood with his nose balanced on Mrs Greychurch's ample lap, his eyes gazing deeply at her.

'And Louisa said something about wings … It was ridiculous really. Sit down, Gregor. The woman clearly doesn't know a thing about horses. Wings, how ridiculous,' rambled Mrs Groves.

'Wings?' said Mrs Greychurch, suddenly paying attention. 'I don't like the sound of that. I saw something with wings the other night.'

Mrs Groves sank slowly downwards in her seat.

'There is something going on,' Mrs Greychurch continued, looking sinister. 'Here, have a lovely biscuit, Gregor, good boy.'

Mrs Groves shuddered. Could her friend suspect her? Did she realise that she, Mrs Groves, had been keeping a secret for years?

'Surely you read those notes I gave you, about my ancestor Sally Lucke, and how she met a terrible end, killed by a sea dragon? ' said Mrs Greychurch with a mad gleam in her eye. 'I tell you now, Estelle Groves, if there is one of those beasts pursuing you, you should take great care. Watch your back. Don't leave the house without a weapon! They are murderous creatures.'

'I can't say I found time to read your notes ...' said Mrs Groves quietly, staring at Gregor, her cheeks flushed crimson. 'After all, it happened a very, very long time ago. I am sure, even if there were some kind of sea dragon, it would be a gentle sort of creature. A little highly strung, perhaps, like a horse ...'

Mrs Greychurch had stopped listening. She threw out her arms and Gregor leaped to his feet with a startled bark.

'It was the night of a terrible storm in the year 1616. Sally Lucke set out in a hurry, just as the sun was setting. According to one account, her younger brother, my ancestor, said she was upset. She had a sense of foreboding perhaps, of something terrible about to happen ...' Here

Mrs Greychurch paused for dramatic effect.

'She was last seen walking along the cliff path. Two men, the farmer John Muddle and your own family ancestor, Joseph Groves, saw that dragon. And each gave the same description of the beast. Exactly the same, mind. What further proof could you want? He is a murderous savage beast, my dear. Oh yes, he is. And now he flies the island again, seeking out his next victim. I, Veronica Greychurch, have seen him with my own eyes!'

Mrs Groves edged towards the patio doors leading through to the cafe, tugging Gregor, murmuring, 'Must run, lots to do.'

Gregor watched Mrs Greychurch, fascinated, as she continued, '... And the dragon ate Sally, in one gulp. Her poor little gold ring lay at the top of the cliffs, all that remained of her, poor girl.'

She stared beyond Mrs Groves, with glazed eyes. 'I will avenge her terrible death,' she whispered.

'Well,' said Mrs Groves uncomfortably, her hand on the door, 'I have never seen a dragon flying around and I am outside in all weathers with Gregor and my horses.'

Gregor looked at her. There was at least some truth in this. It was amazing how truthful people could be if they lied carefully.

A cold wind with edges like daggers blew from the north.

'I know who the smuggler was, I'm sure it was Joseph Groves,' said Isabel to herself, for about the tenth time. 'But he's dead and … ouch.' The sword cut, though not deep, was stinging.

She walked across the grassy field by the cliffs, making her way along West Weares, her feet sinking into the long, mushy grass. She had seen the smuggler clearly despite the shadows and she was certain she knew him, he was unforgettable. He was Joseph Groves from the painting at Groves Farm, a man who had lived and died hundreds of years ago, walking around with a sword. He had tried to kill her. Isabel shuddered. She had not planned to travel through time to meet smugglers. She wanted to find the sea dragon and the Maydew witch. She closed her eyes, listening to the sea crashing on to rocks far below her, to the seagulls calling high above. She wondered about John Lucke, whether she could have helped him if she had reacted faster.

She felt eyes watching her. 'Sea dragon?' whispered Isabel.

There was a roar of thunder and lightning flickered overhead, cutting crisply through the sky. The ground trembled beneath her feet and a small rainbow bridged the clouds that scuttled above her. Then, as if someone had taken a paint brush and swept it across the landscape, it was shiny and bright all around her. Isabel could hear an early skylark trilling high above. The grey sky had vanished. In its place was a deep winter blue. Looking back towards home, she saw that the buildings and mobile phone mast had gone, replaced by a cottage. It was a ramshackle building, with a low thatched roof, built from slabs of limestone cut haphazardly into different sizes, and painted white. The small windows had tiny square panes. From the front of the cottage jutted a porch with a hole in the roof and a large wooden door.

A young woman was working among the plants in front of the cottage. Dressed in a long skirt and blouse with an apron over the top, she was hardly taller than Isabel. She hummed loudly to herself as she worked. Isabel approached the woman slowly, not wanting to alarm her. She had a nice face, thought Isabel, friendly.

'What in God's name are you?' said the woman. 'What now? Are you a Demon?' She looked Isabel up and down curiously. 'Where did you come from? What strange stuff you wear. You are no child such as I have ever seen.'

She walked around Isabel, looking at her closely, sizing her up.

'I came …' Isabel pointed behind, lost for words, '… from over there.'

The young woman seemed to be collecting her thoughts. 'Well, you are a strange apparition, that is for sure. And the very image of my own daughter, Rian. You have her eyes and her manner. What is your name, child?'

'Isabel.'

'Indeed?' The woman considered this for a moment. 'Well, I am Agnes Maydew, and if you were from around here, you would know me. All the islanders know me and fear me. They do not wander here by happenchance. Nor speak as you do. So that in itself tells me much. Someone sent you, perhaps. My dear cousin Sally likes to test me for fun. Is this her doing?'

Isabel gasped. Sally, she thought, the smugglers had talked about Sally Lucke. They had killed her father. Agnes Maydew and Sally Lucke, the names from her dragon book. Isabel felt certain that at last she was moving closer to the sea dragon.

Agnes walked in a circle around Isabel, considering her again from all directions, as if she expected her to vanish. 'Well, I am not afeared of any ghost, that's for sure. Least of all one that is but a slip of a girl. What can I offer you, child? What do you need from me?'

Isabel shook her head, puzzled.

'People come to me from far and wide for my herbs,' Agnes explained, pointing to the garden where several leafy plants were growing in the bright cold sunlight. 'What ails you, child? Is one of your family sick?'

Isabel thought carefully. 'I need to speak to Sally,' she said finally.

'Is that so?' said Agnes, her expression steely.

Isabel decided to take a chance. She looked steadily into Agnes's clear, intelligent grey eyes. 'I need to talk to Sally about a murder. And a dragon.'

Agnes shook her head slowly. 'It is easy to do harm by meddling in matters, child. So often I am all that stands between mischief and everyone else. Who tells you of the dragon? Who are you?'

Agnes raised her hand to touch her and Isabel stepped back abruptly. She lost her balance, the ground behind her tipping unexpectedly away, and Agnes vanished. Isabel heard a rushing sound, like wings flapping, and the ground shook as something heavy lifted into the sky. Isabel saw a shadow with a long jagged tail, but then it was gone. A single flash of lightning roared from the sky into the sea, blinding her for a second, then a huge clap of thunder made her jump.

Isabel breathed a sigh of frustration. This trip across time had taken her closer to the dragon, she was sure of it. Now she was standing in the field by the cliffs with the cold northerly wind blowing around her, overlooked by the familiar flats of 2011. She shivered, feeling very alone. Clearly Agnes knew about the dragon. Isabel gritted her teeth. She was even more determined now that she would find both Sally and the sea dragon. She would tell Sally about her father's death. Isabel wrapped her scarf around her neck. White snow clouds were gathering across the horizon and the cold made her arms and legs ache as if ice was creeping into her veins.

Sally wandered along the edge of the sea, watching the waves lap gently at the smooth stones. She did not want to return to the cottage. Her father had vanished again, had not been seen since New Year's Day, and her mother was in a bad mood, crying and feeling sorry for herself. Sally heard strange, fascinating music drifting across the sea and for a while it lulled her into a peaceful state of mind. She missed her father. She remembered him being a very different man when she was younger. It was strange that he had not returned home last night. Then she smiled.

'You cannot affect me, mermaid. I know your games,' she called.

'And yet you look ssad, sister,' said a hissing voice. The mermaid was seated on a rock nearby, her long red hair falling in tangles, her turquoise tail draped elegantly across the rock. 'Your ssadness called to me. Lissten to the music and come with me, I will take you into the ssea, I will show you things, the Sspanish shipwrecks, chessts full of gold.'

The mermaid waved to Sally, studying her closely. 'I ssee that you like gold, ssister. Your poverty pains you. Come with me.'

'And never return?' said Sally. 'Always the deal, fair mermaid, is it not?'

'I will give you a gift, ssister,' said the mermaid, smiling. 'I will give you this bag of gold sovereigns, from the treasure chests deep beneath the sea. Ssee, your troubles will be over.' She held out a hand with a sparkling coin.

'It iss yours,' she hissed. 'All these are yours.' She ran the coins through her fingers, a sparkling stream of coins.

Sally watched, as if spellbound by the money. 'Tell me the truth, and do not lie to me, mermaid. What is your price for this?'

'You speak like a merchant, ssister. Think of the value. Imagine how you could live, how grand you could be on the value of this.'

'But I must know what you wish in return, mermaid.'

'My price is ssimple. A child.'

Sally laughed. 'You are ridiculous, mermaid! I have no children. Nor will I ever. I cannot stand the thought of being like my mother.'

The mermaid's face became coldly sinister. 'Then you have nothing to lose, fair Ssally. A ssmall price to ask, an unborn child of your flesh and blood, to live under the ssea as we do. It iss an honour to be offered thiss chance. We will make the child infinitely happy, all thingss will be herss.' The mermaid ran the coins through her fingers, watching Sally's eyes.

'Very well. If you wish to strike a foolish deal, I agree. Give me the gold.' The mermaid jingled the coins in her cold white fingers one last time and tipped them back into the bag. She held out the small leather bag to Sally. Sally hesitated. Agnes had warned her about the mermaid, to have no dealings with her. But what did Agnes know about gold? Sally needed gold. She could not bear another moment without it and the knowledge of what it could buy her. She snatched it quickly from the mermaid's grasp and clutched it to her chest. The mermaid smiled as Sally checked inside the bag. The gold was there, gleaming and real. Agnes was a fool not to trust the mermaid. Sally felt a wave of relief wash over her. Finally, her life would be her own.

'It is yours,' said the mermaid. 'Don't forget our deal.'

Sally ignored her. She held the bag tightly as she walked up the beach, calculating. This gold could buy her more than finery. If she played it well, it could make her the most important lady on the island. It could bring her the husband she wanted but who slipped through her fingers – Joseph Groves, a man who valued money above all else. As she walked through the trees above the cove, her step became purposeful. She headed briskly towards Groves Farm, her heart lighter than it had been for a long time.

As she reached the windmills, hooves sounded behind her and the rider reined in. Joseph looked down at Sally with a cold smile. He removed his hat, but his eyes were laughing at her, taking in the cheapness of her dress and her lack of a cloak. The boy who had been her childhood friend had changed.

'What brings you from over yonder, Sally Lucke?'

Before she could answer, he jumped down from the horse. Although Sally was tall he towered over her, glowering at her with his strange brown eyes.

'I hear your father has gone carousing again. No sign of him I take it?' he asked.

Sally suddenly felt uneasy. Did Joseph know where her father had gone? There was more to Joseph than met the eye now. He had secrets. She would have to be careful, cunning, stay a step ahead of him while striking this deal. She would be his wife, she would lord over the people who had mocked her, become Mrs Sally Groves, lady of the farm.

'Why would you care, Joseph Groves?' she said, and smiled sweetly. He looked taken aback.

'Let us walk quickly then, I have much work to do this

day and I would know why you are heading for the farm,' he said.

'I have come to make an offer to you. You have dallied in my home, talked of placing a ring on my finger and then acted as if you have forgotten your promises. I will not have such games any longer,' said Sally.

Joseph's laughter carried across to the farm where some of his men stopped working to listen.

'So you offer me a dowry now, poor wench that you are! Your father had great riches after all, the drunken old sot.'

Sally hesitated. What did he mean, '*had* great riches'?

'You may laugh, Joseph,' she continued, 'But the men say the farm does poorly. You spend all your profit on your grand high tastes. You buy no sheep for the farm but choose fine fabrics for your clothes. What I offer can buy what you desire.'

She held out her hand full of gleaming sovereigns, the bag tucked away beneath her skirt. Joseph stared at them, amazed, stunned into silence.

'These are lawfully mine, and there are many more. They are yours when we have a firm deal, when the engagement ring is on my finger and promises are kept,' she said.

The men at the farm, despite their efforts, could not overhear exactly what was said, but afterwards John Muddle returned home to tell his wife that Joseph Groves had talked of marriage with the Lucke girl and he had returned to the farm in very high spirits.

The farm had performed poorly that year, but Joseph had slapped his brother-in-law on the back that afternoon and said that their troubles were over. The word of the engagement went around the island quicker than fire.

Agnes walked briskly across the island to Sally's home, as the chilly winter night drew in. It had been unseasonably warm all day, the sun throwing out more heat than was usual in January. Perhaps this weather had roused the sea dragon from his long sleep. Such extremes of warmth and cold in January were dangerous, bringing terrible storms to the island, flooding the village in Chiswell and crashing ships into the powerful waves of Chesil Beach.

The visit from the strange child, Isabel, had worried Agnes as much as the sea dragon. She was clearly not from the local villages, a traveller of some kind. And yet familiar; her grey eyes and light golden brown hair could even make her one of the Maydew family.

Agnes sighed. The child clearly had powers of some kind. She had appeared from nowhere and had then disappeared before Agnes's own eyes. She talked of murder and dragons, knew about Sally, had come to find Agnes. She rubbed her eyes angrily. All these strange things were connected and yet Agnes could not see the connection. It felt as if things were happening so fast that Agnes could not keep up. As she had predicted, the dragon was bringing rapid change.

The Lucke cottage was always in chaos, children everywhere, and Mrs Lucke asleep in her chair. Agnes could understand Sally's dislike for her life there. As she walked, Agnes considered how she would confront Sally. Surely the child was Sally's doing? Yet Agnes had never seen such clothes, in such strange colours, as worn by Isabel.

Agnes became aware of another visitor ahead of her. There were angry voices carrying on the increasingly cold wind. Agnes pulled a shawl around her shoulders and shivered. She recognised the voice as that of Joseph Groves, no less. Agnes walked lightly, warily, and kept within the shadows of the high bushes that surrounded the Lucke cottage.

There was Sally, in her finest blue dress, her eyes sparkling. She turned and smiled triumphantly at Joseph, who was almost hidden from Agnes's view. Joseph handed Sally a small shining object, a ring, with obvious reluctance.

'What of the gold that you promised, Sally? I have much work to do at the farm and the sovereigns would not go amiss …'

'You must wait,' interrupted Sally, 'Until I am sure of you and this promise. The gold is safe, none may find it.' Sally put the ring on her finger and held out her hand to admire it.

Joseph stepped into Agnes's view, dark and angry. He grabbed Sally by the wrist and pulled her away from the cottage.

'Do not play fast games with me. If the gold is not mine by the end of this week, the cottage and the few poor things you hold dear will go up in flames, including your useless mother.'

Children had run out of the cottage, hearing the angry words. Joseph mounted his horse and pulled the animal round to face Sally.

'I will give you until this hour, the day after the morrow,

or I will take the ring, and leave you nothing but charred dust.'

'Don't threaten me, Joseph Groves,' replied Sally, 'Or I will keep the gold and you will see none of it. The islanders know of our engagement and you cannot turn back. You will look a fool. I will say you became afraid of me, had funny turns, like a maid with the vapours, at the thought of marriage. When I finish, even the children will giggle behind their hands and point at you!'

'Let them point. It is you that they will pity, the wench that no one will marry, too clever to be a wife, too poor and ill-educated for anything else.'

Even from the chilly shade of the hedges, Agnes could feel the heat of Sally's fury.

'Poor I may be, but I have powers at my disposal. I may call mermaids and dragons to serve me! Your precious boats will sink in whirlpools, all your goods lying useless on the sea bed. I have a book ...' Sally's voice shook with rage.

'Congratulations!' snarled Joseph. 'It is a shame you cannot read it.'

Agnes stepped deeper into the shade of the hedges as Joseph spurred the horse into a gallop. 'A book,' she whispered to herself. 'I know well which book she has. What is she planning?'

Sally was in trouble, of her own making as usual. No wonder the dragon flew around the island all night like a restless ghost. Sally was plotting and scheming. Agnes wondered how on earth she would be able to prevent disaster befalling them all.

CHAPTER NINE

2 JANUARY 2011

A SUSPECT IS REVEALED

Mrs Groves sat in front of a large fire in the living room knitting happily. The horses were fed and all was well with the world. Even Gregor had settled for a nap, his head resting peacefully on her foot, his shaggy black and white fur neatly brushed. She put on Radio Two, which played organ music at this time of day, but it was company. She shouldn't have eaten that cake, she thought, as she adjusted her waistband to accommodate the extra inch of winter fat. Mrs Greychurch tapped lightly at the window and let herself in at the kitchen door. A blast of cold air came with her.

Mrs Groves sighed to herself. She knew that her friend was often lonely in the evenings, with her daughter Miranda away at school or on expensive trips abroad, spoilt brat that she was. A real minx.

'Shall I put the kettle on, dear?' said Mrs Greychurch. Gregor bounded around her, leaping and barking.

'Yes, do.' Mrs Groves put her knitting down beside the chair and stood up, reluctantly, and found the tea for her. 'Sit down, Gregor. He's such a nuisance! What brings you out this evening, Veronica?' Gregor plonked himself in his bed and looked at them resentfully. He chewed at the edge of his blanket, watching Mrs Groves with round angry eyes.

'I was just thinking about your family history.' Clearly, Mrs Greychurch had decided to make peace after her outburst at the cafe.

'Ah.'

The room suddenly became gloomy, as though dark figures crowded close to Mrs Groves, listening. Gregor whined, looking around. He bit a lump from the blanket and chewed, swallowing it with a gulp. Ghosts made him nervous and hungry. The grandfather clock in the corner ticked slowly. Mrs Groves liked to talk about the Groves family history, but she felt as though there were eyes watching her, from the pictures on the wall, waiting to see what she would say.

Together, the two women felt their own eyes drawn to a portrait in the corner of the room of a dark, handsome man with an arrogant expression, holding a riding whip. 'What is the story about him?' said Mrs Greychurch, peering at the painting over her glasses. 'He's a dashing fellow but rather ... threatening.'

'That's Joseph Groves. I'll fetch my family tree from the dining room,' Mrs Groves replied. As soon as she left, Gregor yanked the blanket from his bed, shook it fiercely, and threw it around the room, growling and rolling in it. He settled beside Mrs Greychurch to chew another hole in the wool.

By the time Mrs Groves returned, she was excited about the subject and didn't notice Gregor gulping lumps of blanket. After all, it was only family history, nothing sinister, people dead and buried, just names on old gravestones.

'As you know,' she said, clutching a pile of papers, 'a few parts of the present house date back to the sixteenth century. It was originally built by the Groves family in the mid 1500s, by Joseph Groves' father in fact. They kept a lot of sheep in those days, as well as farming the land. It was a good farm back then, well run, although I believe it ran into difficult times under Joseph. He liked to spend money and only the finest things would do. Gregor, what are you doing? Why are you making that noise?'

'Ummph,' burped Gregor.

'The finest things, eh?' said Mrs Greychurch, concentrating on Joseph.

'Joseph was excellent with horses. He preferred being out on horseback to managing the farm, but when his father died he had to take over. Then there was a terrible fire. The farmhouse went up in flames.'

'Flames …' said Mrs Greychurch. 'What a terrible death, burning in flames. So he never married? Such a handsome man …'

'Oh no, he survived the fire but was left penniless.' Mrs Groves paused and took a deep breath. She knew she too was playing with fire.

'As for marriage, I wonder if you know the story of his engagement to your own ancestor, Sally Lucke?'

Mrs Greychurch leaped out of her chair as if she had been electrocuted. Gregor dropped the blanket and jumped around her, barking a squeaky startled bark. 'Amazing! Sally Lucke and Joseph Groves!' she exclaimed, her chest heaving with emotion. 'She would have been mistress of all this, the farm, everything.'

Her friend nodded sadly, 'But …'

'But the dragon devoured her!' bellowed Mrs Greychurch. 'A girl in the very prime of her life. Eaten on the brink of marriage and all the joys of family life. He would have made a fine husband.'

'Well, I'm not sure,' said Mrs Groves. 'Joseph has always looked a bit menacing to me. Sally came from a very poor family, the Luckes. Her engagement ended in a matter of days, as she disappeared on the very night of the fire.'

'Murdered …' interrupted Mrs Greychurch.

'An odd engagement. Joseph was known to be fond of money. Why did he plan to marry a girl who was so poor?'

Mrs Greychurch nodded. 'Sally was very beautiful, my dear.' She gazed into space. 'So what became of Joseph after Sally's sudden death? After the terrible fire? No doubt he devoted his life to avenging himself upon the evil dragon that took his one true love?'

'Not quite,' said Mrs Groves. 'At the end of 1616 he received a large sum of money. He rebuilt the farm. The farm records show a large amount of money coming in from a wealthy London lady, gold no less, but none of the documents names her. Gregor, if you make that noise again, I will put you in the kitchen.' Gregor wedged himself behind an armchair and hiccupped.

Mrs Groves continued, 'The story goes that, on the day Joseph received the money, he threw Sally's engagement ring into the sea, saying, "Let the sea have it. The wench has paid in full and I have no further need of it." Legend has it that a mermaid with a turquoise tail caught the ring and kept it.'

Mrs Greychurch snorted. 'A likely story! Mermaids! What imaginations people have!'

Mrs Groves sat up until late in the evening, reflecting on the past. Funny how time flew. It seemed like only yesterday that Gregor was a puppy, curled sweetly in his new basket. Now he stretched out the full length of the rug, his paws twitching as he dreamed, his tummy rumbling like thunder. The silly dog had obviously eaten something he shouldn't. The nice new blanket from his bed had gone, she could not find it anywhere. As she had watched Mrs Greychurch drive away from the farm earlier, she thought she saw a man on horseback. She had caught her breath and wrapped her cardigan tightly around her to protect herself from the ghosts of the past as he vanished into the night.

Now, as the clock struck midnight, Mrs Groves clicked the farmhouse door, shutting Gregor indoors, and tiptoed to the stables. The darkness of the winter night was intense. She could barely see her own hand in front of her. An owl hooted in the old elms and the horses shifted uneasily. She took the broom from the whitewashed wall of the stable, then waited, listening to the silence. She hooked a small bale of straw over her shoulder. Gregor whined from the farmhouse. She sighed. He would be on her bed by the time she got back. The duvet would be chewed at the corners and there would be fur everywhere.

Mrs Groves walked to nearby Church Ope Cove by the narrow footpath through the woods that the old smugglers once used. Ferns brushed her legs and twigs crackled beneath her feet. She took a turning sharp right, where bushes hid wooden steps that led downwards towards the sea. No one but her ever came here, she was sure of it. Mrs Groves was careful not to slip on layers of dead leaves beneath her feet, using the broom to feel the way ahead. It was always cold here, the steps leading to a rocky corner facing south towards Freshwater Bay, less sheltered than Church Ope Cove. Mrs Groves stepped warily. As she reached the rocks, at the entrance to the cave, she ran her hands over the layers of cold limestone that jutted forward and hid the opening. She crouched down. If you knew it was here, the entrance to the cave was easy to find, wide but not high. Once in, she stood up inside the airy cave and switched on the small torch that was in her pocket. As she looked around the empty space, she suddenly felt very alone with her secrets, as though they were a great weight on her shoulders, pressing her down. Tears made her eyes blur and her hands trembled as she clutched the broom.

'Get a grip on yourself,' she said firmly, balancing her torch on a rock.

She swept out the pile of straw that looked like it had been slept in and tossed the fresh straw around the small cave. Every now and then she glanced towards the entrance, hoping that he would come back, wondering where he was. After years of looking after a cosy, sleeping creature, it was strange to be in an empty cave. Mrs Groves sighed. She had never really considered the rights and wrongs of caring for a dragon, until now, when it was too late. It had all seemed very simple. All creatures needed someone to love and look after them.

After all, a dragon was much the same as a horse.

CHAPTER TEN

3 JANUARY 2011

A CONFRONTATION

Mrs Greychurch bustled around before breakfast. She was tidying up, plumping the many multi-coloured cushions and putting flowers in the vases. As she primped some wilted carnations, Miranda sauntered into the room, wearing the latest purple Capri trousers, and threw herself down on the sofa.

'Not there, dear,' said Mrs Greychurch.

'Mrs Groves does some odd things, doesn't she?' said Miranda, throwing various cushions aside. 'You're not going to hoover again, are you?'

'Mrs Groves, dear? Why do you say that? Look how lovely and clean the rug is, lemon juice does that, you know.' Mrs Greychurch straightened the green rug so that it ran exactly parallel to the dusky pink sofa.

'I saw her last night out of the window, heading down to the cove with a broom. Does she fly it down there? I mean, why would anyone need a broom down by the cove? She didn't even have Gregor with her.'

'Didn't have Gregor?' said Mrs Greychurch, astounded. 'Are you sure?'

'She must have one of her animals down there. Strange

55

place for a horse.'

Mrs Greychurch narrowed her eyes. 'I couldn't say,' she spluttered. 'How extraordinary.'

She slammed the wet carnations on the sideboard and snatched up her coat.

'Not hoovering then?' said Miranda. 'I'd like a coffee if that's not too much trouble ...' But her mother had already left the house, her coat flying behind her, heading for the cove.

A fine drizzle of freezing rain fell as Mrs Greychurch clambered down the steps to the beach.

'I know it's here! She's been keeping secrets from me. After all I've done for her!'

She stopped abruptly. 'I see you!' she screamed.

The dragon swooped and landed neatly in front of her. His claws clicked on the stones and he swirled his long tail. He tucked his jagged wings behind his body and leaned towards the frightened woman, tilting his head.

'You evil creature!' she cried.

The dragon snorted and fixed his wide yellow eyes on her, looking puzzled. She ran at the dragon and lashed at his nose with her nails.

'You killed Sally! I know it.'

'Now then, come on, you silly old thing,' said Mrs Groves, scrambling up a slope beside them. 'Let's get you back in your cave. Out of harm's way.'

Mrs Greychurch stared at her friend with her mouth wide open.

'I have been up all night worrying about him. No sign until now. Thank heavens he's back. How clever of you to find him,' rambled Mrs Groves. She had straw stuck in her jumper and looked as though she had slept the night in a stable.

Mrs Greychurch stared from Mrs Groves to the dragon, still speechless. Her mouth opened and shut and no sound came out. The dragon was very still, gazing at her as though transfixed.

'I think he likes you,' said Mrs Groves.

Mrs Greychurch sat heavily on a rock and wiped the cold sweat off her forehead. The dragon edged closer to her, his scales gleaming gold and green in the morning light. Then he curled up into a large ball by her feet and fell sound asleep.

'You certainly have a way with dragons. Perhaps you remind him of someone. He seems to be a very straight-forward sort of animal,' she said, patting his back. 'Now if you just stay here for five minutes and keep an eye on him, I'll get my broom from the cave and we can coax him down there together.'

'Well,' spluttered Mrs Greychurch, then she stopped. She looked down at the dragon. It looked harmless, fast asleep right next to her. Perhaps Mrs Groves was right. Perhaps she had a way with dragons. Mrs Greychurch felt quite proud. She would tell Miranda later. She would tell her about, now what was it …? There were distant voices, singing in the sea, distracting and strange. Beautiful high voices, singing of gold and shipwrecks, the song of the sea. She swayed a little to the music and started to hum.

'If I could just step into the waves, how warm and safe it looks, how cold and lonely it is out here,' she said aloud. The dragon snuffled peacefully.

Mrs Greychurch tried to remember why she was waiting

for Mrs Groves. The song filled her head completely. It had something to do with a dragon. She could hear voices calling out to her. They called, 'Ssally, Ssally.'

She fell soundly asleep, her cheek pressed against the rock, and rain pattering lightly around her, as the mermaid watched and waited, combing her hair and humming to the music of the sea.

'Leave her,' she said to the merpeople. 'I want the young one. Her daughter. Eassier to manage. A finer catch for ssure.'

CHAPTER ELEVEN

A SHIFT IN TIME

ISABEL, SALLY AND THE MERMAID

Isabel jumped neatly out of the bedroom window and landed on the kitchen roof. 'Hah!' she said triumphantly. 'It's easy … Oh no!' In the drizzling rain, the roof was more slippery than she was used to. She surfed from one end to the other and fell into the bush by the back door. 'Drat.'

The bush looked a bit crushed. Isabel rearranged some of the leaves. Luckily her mother had already left for work at the post office in Fortuneswell and Suzie was at her childminder's in Southwell village.

Already soaked, Isabel walked the short distance from her house to the cliffs and stood in the endless rain, waiting, hoping that something would happen. Sometimes she felt as if her whole life was spent waiting for things to happen. Everywhere she went, the dragon was one step ahead of her, tipping her backwards in time, showing her people and places from the past. In the distance she heard strange thin voices, like a choir singing from the sea. The sound made her shudder. If a jellyfish could sing, that was what it would sound like, she thought.

Fifteen minutes later, she was still there, her clothes soaking wet and stuck to her. The strange reedy singing

59

had gone on and on. Her mobile beeped loudly, making her jump. Ben texted to remind her that the salsa class was still on that afternoon and she had promised to go as his partner. Isabel drummed her fingers on the phone. She really could not remember agreeing to that. Ben was always signing her up for things.

Suddenly there was a flash of white hot lightning. Isabel heard dragon wings flapping, drawing closer. A rainbow gleamed in front of her, so close that it seemed to begin just feet away from where she was standing. She gazed into the clear colours, painting the grass below with shimmering red, orange and blue. She reached out to touch the rainbow and, as she did so, the turf beneath her slipped and crashed down the sheer cliff face into the sea. Isabel stepped back, gasping. The landslip revealed steps cut into the stone, leading steeply down the cliffs. The steps were old, deeply worn, as though trodden for hundreds of years, perhaps by smugglers needing a quick route to and from West Bay. They would have landed tobacco and brandy, from Cornwall or even France.

Isabel followed the slippery steps, one by one, looking down nervously towards Blacknor Rock, where the waves lapped. She wobbled. 'Better not look down,' she thought. 'I bet the smugglers took this route at night, when they couldn't see down the cliffs.'

The steps were now so overgrown they must have been hidden for a long time. Gorse bushes and thistles reached across the path. Slowly, Isabel made her way to the foot of the cliffs and jumped from rock to rock to stand on the dark stone of Blacknor Rock. The cold wind and rain blew into her face, but Isabel felt sure she was not alone.

'Welcome, ssister,' said a cold hissing voice. 'No doubt you heard uss ssinging, calling to you.'

'Not really,' said Isabel. 'It just made me feel a bit ssick. Sick, I mean.'

The mermaid was just a few feet away, her skin gleaming white, her eyes an intense clear green, like marbles. When she smiled, she revealed sharp white teeth. 'Welcome,' she said again.

'Who are you?' asked Isabel.

'An old friend, you could ssay. I have come to help you. You sseek Agness. You wait in the rain for her to come.'

'That's right,' said Isabel, reluctantly.

'Sso, what iss your name?' asked the mermaid.

'Isabel.'

'Ah,' said the mermaid, 'A good Maydew name, of coursse. Agness and I are friends, old friendss. I can take you to her. In return for a ssmall favour.'

Isabel felt as if cold hands were running up and down her back. 'What is the favour?'

'I am owed by Ssally Lucke. She planss to run away. Tomorrow, a sstorm comes across the ssea. It brings terrible windss, snow, hail and thunder. The ssea dragon has woken from hiss long sleep. But all will be well if the deal iss kept. Do not protect Ssally. Ssend her back to me.'

The mermaid edged closer to Isabel. 'Promisse me.'

'I'm not making any deals with you. I'll find Agnes myself!'

'Headsstrong! Like Ssally! Like Agness!'

The mermaid lunged at her suddenly, like a shark attacking, with one flex of her tail. She seized Isabel by the hair and yanked her head backwards, pulling her into the sea, and ducking her head into the freezing water. Salt water exploded up Isabel's nose as she struggled. She clenched her fist and hit the mermaid as hard as she could across the ears.

'You're no friend of Agnes,' spluttered Isabel, struggling free.

The mermaid's icy cold hand gripped her arm and held her tightly.

'Ssally will die. Such a wasste. And you with her.'

Isabel wrenched her arm away from the mermaid's tight grasp. She backed away from her, watching the mermaid carefully. The mermaid slipped into the sea, her tail flicking behind her. Relieved, Isabel leaped from rock to rock until she reached the cliff steps.

'Evil creature! I thought mermaids were meant to be lovely!' she exclaimed, rubbing her arm where the mermaid's grip had bruised her.

She followed the steep steps to the top of the cliffs, pausing near the top to catch her breath. The mermaid had gone and, with her, the strange singing. Agnes's ramshackle cottage appeared ahead. Isabel picked up speed, eager to see Agnes. She would ask her again about the sea dragon.

'Who are you?' said a cold voice. There, on the wall in the cottage garden, kicking her legs, was a striking girl in a long blue dress and worn, patched-up brown boots.

'Miranda?' said Isabel, confused. What was Miranda Greychurch doing here in front of Agnes's cottage?

'My name is Sally Lucke, since you ask. Are you some animal? Did my cousin conjure you?' Sally jumped down from the wall. She had an air about her as though she knew everything and you knew nothing.

'No, my cousin could not be so clever. A strange thing you are too. Dripping wet, like seaweed.' Sally studied her as carefully as Agnes had. 'You have a look of Agnes about you. Who are you?'

'You are Sally Lucke!' gasped Isabel.

Irritated, Sally caught Isabel's arm and twisted it behind her back.

'Come now, answer my question. I know who I am. Tell me who you are.'

'It's none of your business,' blurted Isabel. 'Let go of my arm! I have to talk to you about your father, John Lucke.'

Sally stepped back, her expression cold and wary. 'What do you know about my father?'

Isabel took a deep breath. She needed Sally to take her seriously. She thought about the note at the front of her book, 'Sally Lucke, taken by a dragon …'

'I … I read about you, and a dragon.'

'I am more than a match for any dragon, if you mean to threaten me,' said Sally, raising an eyebrow. 'It is but a creature after all, mine to command, if I wish.'

Sally stared intently at Isabel, considering her carefully. 'I wonder what you really know. A strange creature, indeed. I saw you talking to the mermaid. You come here to threaten me, set me from my path. The mermaid has set her price for my gold and a foolish one it is. Or is this Agnes's doing? She would always wish to have a hand in my destiny, so much greater than hers. This is indeed a strange day, there are bad omens …'

Sally shuddered. A bank of glowing white clouds were massing together in the distance over the sea, drawing a silver line across the horizon. The air was much colder than before. A storm was on the way.

'There are always bad omens,' said Isabel glumly. It had been a long day already, with mermaids, scary cliff paths and endless rain. She was soaked, her arm hurt, and there was no dragon.

Sally suddenly smiled down at her. 'So Agnes tells me, in much the same voice,' she said, amused. Her face lit up and her eyes sparkled. 'But I never listen to other people, what does she know? It is time to find my own way!'

For the first time, Isabel felt that she should trust Sally 'The dragon …' she said.

'Hah, bad omens and dragons!' sneered Sally. 'Serpents are no longer feared in these modern days. Value and profit are what matter most. In these new fangled times, our will to do what we wish is more important than the old magic. Dragons and mermaids! The days will come when none believes in such creatures.'

Sally laughed. 'I long to see what my high and mighty cousin makes of my new life when I am wed. She will fall into step behind me, sure enough. I am weary of her high-handed ways with me.'

A ring on her finger sparkled, catching Isabel's eye. 'I am engaged, as you see, to Joseph Groves. When I was but eight years old and he twelve years, he swore that we would be wed and I would have the most beautiful dress in the island. He said that none would stop him, he would send for the best cloth from France. I would not have to sweep and clean as I do at home, nor sit late by the door waiting for my father to return,' said Sally.

'It's a very pretty ring,' said Isabel.

'It will be a great match, though it was not an easy task to arrange. I insisted on the ring. It is beautiful, far better than the ugly coins he awaits so eagerly. Perhaps he should wait a bit longer …'

Isabel shifted uneasily from one foot to the other.

'I do not trust him,' Sally added suddenly.

'You are right not to,' said Isabel. 'Your father has been killed. He saw the smugglers and confronted them. Joseph told his men to kill him and they threw him into the sea, into Deadman's Bay. I heard them.'

Sally looked at her, her eyes widening and her expression changing from disbelief to fury. 'Are you sure of this? Sea demon, if you lie to me, I will throw you back to the mermaid!'

'You know I am telling the truth,' cried Isabel. 'You can't marry Joseph because he is a liar and a murderer!'

'He will pay for this,' said Sally, shoving Isabel out of her way.

Chapter Twelve

3 January 1616

An Approaching Storm

'For Heaven's sakes, what are you doing in my garden, head to toe in mud?' exclaimed Agnes.

'I slipped,' said Isabel, struggling to her feet. She had fallen flat on her back when Sally pushed her and was now dripping with mud, as well as sea water from her struggle with the mermaid.

'Then take more care in future,' said Agnes, and shifted her attention anxiously to the horizon. 'I fear there is trouble ahead for us. I cannot say how or why. The plague comes and goes, but now I feel there is a storm coming, bringing more change. These have been difficult years for us on the island, Isabel.'

Isabel rubbed her muddy hands nervously together. 'I have read about the plague,' she said.

'Then you are fortunate, for many lives have been lost. I have had no time to read about it,' said Agnes.

'And the King is, umm … ?' added Isabel.

'King James, of course, as surely you know. The islanders would lay down their lives for the King, as they would for good Queen Elizabeth before him, a just Queen. But now the puritans dressed in black come to the island and tell us God is displeased. None may drink or smile, for fear of offending them. They carry bibles everywhere and God's word is what they say and none other.'

'I expect people find you a little … different,' said Isabel.

'Changes in the world affect me greatly. Now my work is held in less esteem. There is much talk of evil spirits and curses,' said Agnes. 'In the village, they hang witch stones above their doors to protect them. Witch stones! I aid with the spinning and the gathering of the harvest over at Groves Farm, and they are grateful, but few of them will come to me. I know what they call me. The Maydew witch!'

'Of course! The Maydew witch!' said Isabel, delighted. 'Of course, that's who you are! I heard about you. Everyone has heard of you! Even hundreds of years from now.'

Agnes frowned at her. 'And there are those like my cousin Sally who live before their time. She asks too many questions and is restless. She does not respect the old ways or belong to the new world. I fear for her.'

Isabel looked at Agnes. 'Just now, I met Sally. I tried to talk to her about her father and I tried to tell her she's in danger. She plans to be married and …'

Agnes held up her hand. 'Who knows what Sally plans. Sally has more sides to her than a cut jewel and she is as hard. Her life has made her hard. There is more in her mind these days than high romance. She dreams of power and wealth and despises all who do not share her dreams. Yet we must let events run as they will.'

Isabel looked puzzled, 'So you would do nothing? Even if Sally dies?'

Agnes thought this over for so long that Isabel felt she had been forgotten.

'When we set events in motion, we must face the result. That is the basis of all magic – cause and effect. No need for candles or magic circles. Sally knows magic as well as I. She has grown impatient with the simpler life; there is little I can do to turn her, for she will not listen to me. If, as you say, you spoke to her, then the turn of events may rest with you.'

'I don't know if she believed me,' said Isabel.

'Then why are you here? It seems clear to me that you flit across time at your will. You are not of this time. That is powerful magic. You will change how things happen.'

'I don't know anything about magic.'

'Sometimes the future frightens *me*, Isabel. Who knows what will become of our people and their simple ways? I hear tell of vast new lands over the seas, the Americas, they call them. Perhaps it is time to consider what you do know.'

'I know that I need to find the sea dragon, and to help Sally,' said Isabel. Now that I have found the Maydew witch, she added to herself.

Agnes suddenly held out her hand and pressed it against Isabel's forehead. Her wrist smelled of lavender. Isabel felt her shoulders relax. Her eyes closed.

'The sea dragon is not of our time. He belongs to the old ways. You would do better to fear him,' said Agnes quietly. 'Yet if you would see him, if that is why you are here, I will show you.'

Just then rain started to fall around them and a heavy swirling mist descended. Isabel felt Agnes's fingers slipping away. She sank on to the grass of the cottage garden, listening to the waves beating against the cliffs, a soft sound that became the steady beat of wings, dragon wings. Isabel kept her eyes closed. Perhaps if she did not try to look for him, this time he would draw close and she would be able to see him. A white light flashed and thunder groaned. Isabel imagined the sea dragon, his scales shimmering with gold and green. She thought about how it might feel to be very ancient, to have been alive all these years, and always to be alone. She imagined herself moving through time with him. She glimpsed an unfamiliar island with croft-like cottages scattered around. She felt how gentle the sea dragon was and how fragile, too, the people around her were. She felt like a small wave on the sea. But surely even a small wave was significant. She saw a figure falling, tumbling into the stormy sea, and high above on the cliffs, a man watching.

Isabel opened her eyes to find herself alone in the driving rain of a winter storm. 'It's Joseph Groves,' she exclaimed. 'He's going to kill her. He's going to kill Sally Lucke.'

The rain streamed down her face like rivers of icy cold tears.

CHAPTER THIRTEEN

3 JANUARY 2011

THE LETTER

Mrs Groves was sorting through the attic. Gregor had bounded up the steps after her and was now nose deep in an old box, sneezing loudly. 'Be quiet, Gregor, I can't think. Don't chew the box. No, leave it, let it go.' She tried to take the box away. He growled at her in a low playful growl.

'You silly dog, I didn't come up here to play tug of war!' Gregor shook the box and bounced backwards, his tail bobbing up and down.

'Sit! Or you will have to go back down the ladder.' Gregor sank on to his haunches, disappointed. He whined gently, gazing at Mrs Groves with sad round eyes.

It was freezing in the attic this evening, as a thin coating of snow landed lightly on the roof above her. The rain that had fallen in torrents earlier had frozen into silvery sheets, and the snowstorm was finally on its way, just as the TV forecast had promised. Mrs Groves pulled on a pair of woollen gloves as she felt her hands going numb. She worked her way under the low roof into the far corner, using her torch to find the wooden beams. This part of the building was so old she felt sure she would go through the floor at any moment. Gregor sneezed loudly and dust flew up all around them.

'Gregor, why can't you leave things alone for five minutes?'

She made a random choice, a bulging box in the far corner, and dragged it out towards her. She perched her torch on a beam nearby and tugged the box open. Papers slid out and cascaded on to the attic floor. Gregor wheezed beside her.

'Why don't you go down, you silly dog? You shouldn't be up here with your allergies.'

She leafed through the piles of paper. Most of this could be thrown out, she could fill several black bags with all the paperwork up here. Mrs Groves sighed. She hated tidying up and the attic had needed sorting out for donkey's years. There were several letters and piles of old accounts for the farm.

She pulled out a very old note on which someone had scrawled, '*Do not pay the men in full. Reduce by one third*'. It was signed by Joseph Groves. The edges were burned as if the account had survived a fire. Someone had then carefully added up figures to make a fine total of sovereigns.

Then there was a piece of stiff folded paper, with brown age spots. She opened it carefully and read aloud.

4 January 1616

Deare Agnes

Cousine, feare not for me. I have made a decisione of much consequence and Mother must fende for Herself. 'Tis not my job to kepe her now Father is gon, God only knows where he rests, God blesse his soul. I have made

71

poore choices of late and cannot remain on the islande. Sadly, I must flee tonighte.

Mrs Groves shuddered. Cold air blew across her as if a ghost were reading over her shoulder. She glanced behind her nervously. Mrs Groves unfolded the lower part of the letter.

I will forward to you Monies to care for my Familie and to improve matters for Yourselfe. Beware Joseph Groves for he intendes Harme. Yet He will know the Error of this shortly when I have Returned his Precious Ring. Your Devoted Cousine, Sally Lucke.

'How extraordinary,' said Mrs Groves, 'Written just before she died, poor girl.'

A mouse ran along the beam beside her and Gregor hurtled towards her in a panic, toppling piles of boxes and knocking the torch over. 'For goodness sakes! It was just a mouse!' She could feel Gregor's anguished eyes on her in the darkness.

'A mouse, not a hedgehog – they live outside.' She felt Gregor relax. He leaned against her, panting and wheezing.

'Why must you make everything so complicated? I can't even tidy up the attic!' Gregor licked her face happily.

'I don't have any biscuits up here. We will have to go downstairs.'

Mrs Groves sat back on her heels and thought about the past. She remembered her grandmother's smile, the cottage garden in the sunshine, the scent of lavender.

Gregor whined and scratched at the loft hatch.

Mrs Groves sighed.

The snow was starting to freeze as the afternoon slid into evening and the temperatures dropped impossibly low. A few snowflakes fell in light sprinkles like silver dust. Thin sheets of ice formed on the greenish-grey sea. Isabel sat on her bed, watching the sun slide behind the clouds and drop below the horizon. She tried to imagine what Sally had done next, all those years ago. Had Joseph Groves killed Sally? What had happened to the dragon? She stared outside, looking for an answer in the sinister surface of the sea.

'You look all nobble,' said Suzie from the doorway, dressed in a tea towel.

'What?' said Isabel.

'You know, like a nobble princess.'

'Noble.'

'That's what I said,' said Suzie.

'Have you seen Miranda?' their mother shouted up the stairs. 'Mrs Greychurch is on the phone. She went out hours ago and isn't back yet.'

'No,' called Isabel. 'I saw her the other day at the farm, with Gregor, but not since then.'

'Mrs Greychurch says can you nip over and look for her? She's watching a film that doesn't finish until 5 p.m. and it will be dark by then. Miranda went to Church Ope Cove for a walk.'

Isabel sighed. She and Miranda were not exactly enemies,

but they were not friends either.

Then a slow creepy feeling that Miranda was in danger swept over her, like a wave. 'The mermaid!' exclaimed Isabel. 'Sally made a deal with the mermaid. And Sally and Miranda look like sisters! What if she's met the mermaid at Church Ope Cove?'

'Have you been eating the fish food again?' said Suzie.

Isabel threw open her bedroom window.

'I'll tell,' said Suzie, narrowing her eyes.

'I'll take you next time, when you're dressed,' said Isabel.

'I'm dressed now,' called Suzie after her. 'You just squashed that bush, jumping on it like that.'

'See you later. And don't shout.'

'Ok,' shouted Suzie from the window. She whipped off the tea towel and pressed her bottom firmly against the window, leaving a heart-shaped print.

Miranda perched on a rock at the edge of the sea at Church Ope Cove, feeling comfortable, her long legs twisted together. The air sparkled with frost, clear and perfect, while tiny snowflakes cascaded around her. Miranda smiled and stretched her legs out in front. 'Funny things, legs,' she thought, 'Ugly, awkward things. I wish I had a tail, like a fish.'

She watched the tiny snowflakes glisten as they settled

on her. In the distance, faint music twinkled across the sea, as though tiny bells were ringing. Miranda felt a wave of sadness run through her. She sighed. How hard it was to go backwards and forwards, from her school in Sherborne to the island. Her friends at boarding school were different to her. She did not fit in anywhere. She wished there were somewhere she completely belonged. The music became clearer, moving closer.

Miranda thought about how she often felt lonely. How lovely the sea seemed, all that deep turquoise darkness. The sea was more real than any other part of her life. Miranda found herself swaying slightly. There was singing, the most beautiful voices she had ever heard.

In the sea, the last of the winter light flashed in the icy waves. Fish, she thought vaguely, as a large fish tail flicked up into the air. Beautiful hands with long white fingers reached out of the water and grasped a rock. The girl who lifted herself out of the sea turned and smiled at Miranda. She had long shimmering red hair that reached to her waist. 'A mermaid,' gasped Miranda entranced.

'Daughter of Ssally Lucke, we have an arrangement, ssister.'

Around her, tails plunged in and out of the waves. Arms waved to her. The mermaid smiled at her. The splash of the waves made her feel dreamy, half asleep. The mermaid beckoned. Miranda closed her eyes as the music ran through her. She climbed down from the rock and waded into the sea, which felt amazingly warm.

The water closed behind her leaving barely a ripple and snow sprinkled lightly on the sea like a fine dusting of icing sugar.

Isabel had barely made it to the end of her garden path before the rescue of Miranda went wrong. First, Gregor had bounded into the garden, nearly knocking her flat and covering her with mud and snowy paw prints.

'Don't encourage him, Isabel,' said Mrs Groves. 'I am trying to train him not to jump up.'

Mrs Groves dismounted from Isaac at the gate, handing Isabel the reins. 'I had better put Gregor on the lead. You've over-excited him.' Gregor was rolling wildly on the lawn, snow landing on his white fluffy stomach.

'Does your mother know that Suzie is making rude gestures at an upstairs window?'

'I have to go, Mrs Groves, Miranda is in danger, there's a mermaid, in the sea …', said Isabel.

'Don't be silly, dear. There are no such thing as mermaids,' said Mrs Groves calmly. 'And Miranda hates swimming. You must have imagined it. Take Isaac for a little ride back to the stables while I chat to your mother. I haven't seen her since Christmas. We're planning a sing-song.'

Isaac eyed them, showing the whites of his eyes. It had been a dull day in the stables and he was ready for a little excitement.

'But it's dark, Mrs Groves, it's snowing …'

As if that wasn't bad enough, Ben had then rolled up, his ears plugged into his MP3 player. 'Here, Izzie, listen to this one, it's Solar Enemy. You missed the salsa class, it was great. I wouldn't worry about Miranda. She likes to do her own thing. A mermaid? Did you also see a werewolf and a vampire tap dancing down the cliffs? Ok, I'll come with you, but I think you're …'

'Move!' hissed Isabel. They both mounted Isaac who shot off at a canter along the footpath behind the Westcliff houses, towards the east of the island, with the two of them sat on his back. Isabel clung on to his mane as Isaac accelerated into a gallop.

'Listen to this one, it's the Red Hot Chilli Peppers and *Under the Bridge* – great melody, I can play this on the guitar,' Isabel heard behind her as they thundered along. They crossed the main road and cut along Gypsy Lane, heading for the footpath that ran right across the middle of the island, towards Church Ope Cove. They flew past the windmills, which stuck up like stumpy thumbs in the dark. Isaac startled at a bramble as they reached the trees at the top of the footpath down to the cove and leaped sideways, finally sliding to a halt, throwing his head from side to side. Isabel jumped to the ground and led him down the twisting path through the snow-laden trees. 'Do horses normally go that fast?' gasped Ben, clutching the front of the saddle and finally unplugging his MP3.

'He's saved us a lot of time. Miranda could be in real trouble.'

'Yeah, I know, but I don't understand why we are

bothering to rescue her,' said Ben bleakly. 'She's always horrible to us.'

The horse slipped and slithered along the steep icy paths. The high chestnut trees had kept most of the snow away from the ground, holding the heavy whiteness in their creaking boughs. From a dark crevice in an old oak, Isabel saw an owl's eyes blinking at them. It was getting darker and shadows loomed. They heard the swoosh of sea below them, as the waves rolled in and out across the pebbles of the cove. Sometimes Isabel thought she heard voices behind them, as if they were being followed. When she looked over her shoulder, she saw tiny lights flitting between the trees, like glow worms.

They slid on the snowy slopes by the pirate graves, set into the side of the hill by ruined St Andrew's church. The huge stone tombs were very old, the lettering on them worn and weathered. Ben peered down at a grave: 'John Ayles, died 1710. That's a long time ago. This place gives me the creeps.'

'Don't think about it,' said Isabel. The rectangular graves had thick stone slabs on top that looked like they could lift at any minute, cold hands pushing beneath them. Towering on the edge of the hill ahead, Rufus Castle was a black shadow against the sky.

'What if there are ghosts? I might be able to take a photo with my mobile,' said Ben, rummaging in his pockets. Isaac snorted, as if to say there are worse things around here than ghosts.

As they reached the narrow steps that led down behind the beach huts to the cove, Isaac startled again at a noise, refusing to go any nearer the sea. He lurked behind one of the ruined walls of the old church.

'It's really dark,' said Ben. 'I can't see my hands.'

'I'll tie him up here,' said Isabel. Music drifted towards them from the sea.

'What amazing music,' said Ben, dreamily.

'What?' snapped Isabel. 'That awful singing jellyfish noise?' She pulled her woollen hat down firmly over her ears and yanked at Ben's hat. He was wearing his mother's stripy hat with tassels at the sides. It now covered his eyes as well as his ears. 'Don't listen to the music.'

'The music isn't a problem. Not being able to see *is*.'

They ran down the sloping beach, slipping across the icy rocks, leaving Isaac swaying happily behind them. He loved music. From the dark trees that surrounded the church, tiny faces peered out and wings fluttered, as the fairies waited to see what would happen. The Southwell fairies were intrigued. Like the merpeople, they were well aware of the deal that had been made between Sally Lucke and the mermaid for gold. Sally had never had a daughter of her own, but there were descendants from Sally Lucke's brothers, Miranda Greychurch the last of the line. Now the fairies waited eagerly to see what would happen.

An icy mist drifted across the water. In the distance the foghorn started to sound at the Bill, sending an eerie low boom across the sea, drowning out the strange twinkling music. Snow fell in white cascades. 'There she is,' shouted Ben, 'I can see someone in the water!'

As they strained their eyes to see through the mist, an arm reached out of the water. A face turned to gaze at them. Beside the mermaid, Miranda swam happily out to sea.

'Phone the coastguard!' said Isabel.

'Are you kidding,' said Ben, 'I am not telling the coastguard there's a mermaid out there. My dad volunteers with the coastguards, I would never hear the end of it.'

Out at sea, there was a sparkle of greenish gold light like a small burst of fireworks. Miranda was thrown in a loop high into the air by a long jagged tail. She crash-landed in shallow water.

'Did you see that?' shouted Isabel. 'Wait here, I'll try and grab her!' She waded into the freezing waves, her legs getting colder and colder. She gasped for breath as the chilly water splashed against her. Miranda seemed to be trying to swim out to sea again, following the mermaid, but luckily the waves were washing her back towards the shore. Isabel grabbed Miranda's foot and tugged her. Miranda struggled and yelled.

'Do you want a hand? Or we could just leave her!' called Ben. Isabel gritted her teeth and yanked a struggling Miranda out of the sea and on to the stony beach. She fell exhausted on to the stones beside Miranda, her legs frozen and numb.

Ben poked her. 'Are you all right?' he said.

'Mmm,' said Isabel.

'Of course she's all right, I'm the one who's not all right!' snarled Miranda. 'What were you playing at, dragging me into the sea?'

From the woods behind them, Isabel felt sure she heard ringing laughter.

'Just wait 'til my mother hears about this,' said Miranda, staggering to her feet and stamping unsteadily up the beach. Seawater cascaded off her in torrents and ice sparkled in her hair, freezing into jagged spikes.

'We rescued you!' said Ben.

'Here, have my jumper,' said Isabel.

'Get lost,' said Miranda, 'It's not even cold!'

'That's very strange,' said Ben. 'You know, even a hairy mammoth would have frozen solid out there tonight. She's just weird.'

Miranda walked stiffly away from them, muttering under her breath.

'She looks like a frozen sea urchin,' said Isabel.

'More like a fish finger. They're such a nice family,' said Ben sarcastically. 'I bet Mrs Greychurch has ice flowing though her veins like Miranda. A family trait.'

'It is funny how Miranda always seems to be drawn to the sea. Something calls her,' said Isabel.

'Stupidity?' said Ben.

Out at sea, a long white arm reached out of the water. With a final flash of tail, the mermaid disappeared.

'Did you see the sea dragon?' said Isabel.

'Oh, we're back to that one, are we?' said Ben.

'Well, you just saw a mermaid!'

'Nope, I may have seen a dolphin, now you mention it,' said Ben.

'No way!' said Isabel. 'It was a mermaid. You know it!'

'I don't want to think about what I saw,' said Ben. He jammed his MP3 player back on.

Somewhere out there was the sea dragon. It had rescued Miranda, throwing her clear of the mermaid. Isabel strained her eyes but could not see the creature in the darkness. Isaac whinnied at them from the ruined church. The foghorn was making him nervous and there were strange tiny voices behind him in the woods. He was keen to leave.

Isabel and Ben followed Miranda back up to the churchyard, where Isaac seemed very happy to see them. He let them mount without his usual sideways skips and wound his way through the trees at a steady pace, looking edgily from side to side in case one of the little strangers lurked there. However, he seemed calmer, as though he was enjoying his adventure. He looked with interest at the shadows and stopped a couple of times to pull at bits of frosted grass beside the path.

'Come on, Isaac,' said Isabel. He trotted briskly, throwing his head up impatiently.

'Are we going the right way?' asked Ben. 'I don't recognise this bit. Miranda went left, but we turned right back there and I think we're heading north now along the edge of the sea, instead of inland. That's The Grove up ahead. What was that funny light? It hurt my eyes, it was so bright, like lightning. And those coloured lights over the trees – is that a rainbow? Did you hear thunder?'

'Oh no,' said Isabel. 'I think something strange is happening.'

'No change there then,' joked Ben, but his usual coolness seemed to have evaporated.

The top of the Grove cliff loomed over them to the left in a heavy dark line. They were too low now to turn inland, following a sandy, overgrown path that ran zigzagging between the cliffs and the sea, with prickly bramble bushes on both sides. It was too narrow to turn back or even see where they were going. Up above them on the edge of the cliffs, a figure holding a lantern appeared with another taller man. The light flashed a few times. Out at sea, they saw a light flash in response from a dark vessel, barely visible above the horizon.

'The French ship is in. Send a boat out for the merchant. Tell him Joseph Groves has business to discuss with him. There will be gold tomorrow evening to cover the goods.'

Startled by the unexpected voice, Isaac thundered up another path through heavy bracken that led steeply away from the voices. Isabel and Ben hung on tightly as he leaped over the bushes that hung across his path, eager now to find his way back.

'Let's get you home,' said Isabel, and Isaac took off at a canter. He knew where he was now, heading inland towards Groves Farm, and he was looking forward to a warm stable and some hay.

'This is odd,' said Isabel to Ben, as they bedded Isaac down. 'The farmhouse looks different. It looks smaller.'

'I can barely see,' replied Ben. Tiny icicles hung from his lashes.

Heavy footsteps clumped past the stable and the door to the farmhouse banged shut. Ben and Isabel waited for the familiar bark. Nothing.

'Mrs Groves *must* be home by now. Where's Gregor?' said Isabel, uneasily.

'She's drinking sherry with your mother and singing *Rule Britannia*, I expect,' said Ben. 'That's what she usually does. I bet Gregor is under the kitchen table with his paws over his ears.'

The upstairs gabled windows had vanished. The building looked more like a barn, long and low, with just two latticed windows downstairs. There was candlelight flickering in one of the windows. A tall figure strode out of the darkness and kicked off boots by the door before entering.

Isabel crept to the window and looked in. There was a roaring fire in the fireplace. It made Isabel shiver out in the cold. Sprawled in a chair by the fire was a dark, brooding man. Even sitting still, he seemed to glow with energy and danger. He stared angrily into the fire. At the table, another man was counting out gold coins into neat piles. A lantern rested on the table beside him, no longer lit. 'Count them again,' said the man in the chair. 'That figure is not what I expected.'

The man looked at him nervously. Joseph was well known for his impatience with people who made mistakes. 'You would that I recount?' he asked.

'Is the Pope a Catholic, my careful brother-in-law? Do not ask foolish questions. Recount,' snarled Joseph. The man seemed offended. He was far more simply dressed than Joseph in a plain black outfit. His face was thin and pale. He laid out the coins and started to count again.

'Times are changing. The King's men are on our tails. I run greater risks and would have more to show for my labour. I pay the men too well. Reduce their cut by a third.'

The man at the table looked alarmed. 'The men will not leave their homes for so little,' he said. 'There is much talk in the village of witchcraft. People are fearful. A flying monster has been seen over the fields, a terrible omen. It is God's hand. He comes to punish the ungodly, for their love of gold and drink.'

Joseph snorted with laughter.

'The people say that Agnes has put the evil eye on them,' continued the anxious-looking man, his fingers twitching. 'Witches are being burned on the mainland these days. The islanders look to you and ask questions when you ride the island at night. They say you are in league with the devil. The men are fearful, superstitious. You spend too well and the local people resent it, the farm does not produce enough to cover luxuries. Nor does … your other business.'

'It is tough indeed. I should marry well, as you did,' Joseph laughed at his brother-in-law, who looked uncomfortable.

'Yet you are promised to Sally Lucke, I hear. The locals fear her, for she is a witch who consorts with demons.'

Joseph rose from the chair and lent across the other man. 'A promise is worth naught. Do not gossip of this, puritan. Mind well, she has a dowry of some great value. I have arranged purchases with the French merchant and will collect the gold from her shortly. When she parts with the gold, I will decide how to deal with her, the ungrateful devious wench.'

The man looked up at him nervously, then resumed counting. He was glad that his wife was so quiet, unlike her brother, Joseph. Sometimes, though, he wished that he had married elsewhere, for though this match had brought him status, it had also brought him too close to Joseph and his dangerous smuggling activities.

'I do not see the purpose in marriage unless there is some use to it,' said Joseph. 'I do not want some snivelling wench and her hopeless family hanging around my kitchen.'

'Your sister and I find much happiness in our marriage,' said the man primly.

Joseph laughed and started to speak, but the words faded as he saw a sudden movement at the window. He kicked back the chair and flew for the door, catching Isabel before she had time to run. Isabel ducked as he snagged a piece of her hair.

'Run,' Isabel shouted to Ben in the stable.

'Spying on me …' snarled Joseph through gritted teeth, yanking Isabel backwards.

'Ow!' she yelled, kicking him hard in the shins.

Joseph curled over in pain. 'You vicious, evil …'

Isabel ran to the stable and found Ben, who was leaning calmly against the stable wall, fiddling with his MP3. 'I can't wait to get home,' he sighed, 'I'm starving and my battery is low.'

'I'm not sure how to tell you this, Ben, but home is a very long way away. It may take a long time to get there.'

'You aren't kidding!' said Ben. 'At least half an hour! My feet are frozen. You really wound up whoever was in the farmhouse. Has Mrs Groves got a boyfriend at last? Who's that man running towards us?'

Isabel grabbed Ben's arm and pulled him after her. They ran along the footpath that led south away from the farm. She felt like she was running in a dream, a timeless place, surrounded by the whiteness of the snow and the heavy darkness of bushes, then finally they reached Weston Street and a few small dark cottages. There were no lights anywhere, as if the whole island slept. She glanced over her shoulder towards the farmhouse. For a second, she saw a line of fire against the sky, white hot, as if a building had gone up in flames. The fire reached into the sky and, silhouetted against the flames, Isabel glimpsed the shape of a flying dragon. There was a flash of lightning and thunder growled in the distance. She blinked and the flames vanished.

They trudged onwards, their feet caked with snow. Familiar houses now lined the road ahead in the village of Weston. Isabel noticed the telephone cables and satellite dishes of 2011. She smiled to herself. She had not looked forward to explaining to Ben that they were lost hundreds of years in the past.

It felt strange being back in the modern world. Isabel felt like she and Ben were the only people alive. How strange that the people she had spoken to from the past, Agnes, Sally and Joseph, were now almost forgotten. They were ghosts, but less than ghosts, for no one but Isabel saw or heard them. She shivered, longing for something bright and real in her life, a creature thousands of years old, who was travelling across time one step ahead of her. Isabel wished for the sea dragon more than she had ever longed for anything in her life.

CHAPTER SIXTEEN

PAST AND PRESENT COLLIDE

ISABEL CONFRONTS JOSEPH

Isabel awoke very early from long strange dreams. She remembered flashes of green and gold, a sword and dark, icy seawater. She rubbed the misty pane of the bedroom window and looked out on to a bleak day. Still dark, she could see that some of the snow had melted overnight leaving dirty piles of slush. The streetlights had an eerie yellow glow. It felt like the last day ever, as if it would never be light again. It felt like the end of everything.

Light footsteps padded to the bathroom. Suzie was already awake. Isabel sighed. Suzie only seemed to need six hours sleep and then she was on the rampage. There was a murmur of voices as Suzie trotted into her mother's room. Isabel knew she didn't have long, quarter of an hour, before Suzie got bored and came looking for her. She had to go now.

She threw open the window and looked down at the dismal hydrangea bush. The kitchen roof below her glistened with frost like an ice rink. 'No way,' she thought and quietly closed the window again.

The house was silent and cold, the only sound the slow ticking of the grandfather clock in the hallway. Isabel tiptoed down the winding staircase from her room, the old stairs creaking loudly under her woollen socks, her coat tucked under her arm. As she headed quietly through the back door and out into the cold morning, she glanced nervously up at her bedroom window. There was no light, no face at the window. Isabel suddenly felt that she might never see Suzie again. She stopped with her hand on the gate, feeling the slippery ice melting under her warm fingers.

Then, without looking back again, she walked away, wading through the dirty snow, in the sickly yellow light. She thought about Sally, confident, brash and determined, soon to die at the hands of Joseph Groves. She thought about Agnes Maydew, how the islanders called her the Maydew witch, although Agnes did her best to help them. And somewhere out there, just beyond her view, was the sea dragon, beautiful and mysterious. She had to see the creature. Just once.

Miranda had also woken up early, from dreams of mermaids and dragons, so vivid they could have been real. After tossing and turning for an hour, she wheeled her bicycle out of the garage and set off. She could not resist the urge to be close to the sea, to smell and touch the water. The sun was slowly rising in the east, throwing out rays of misty yellow light. Miranda pedalled through the slushy snow, along Weston Street and then into the

Westcliff footpaths. She could just see the top of the old white lighthouse to the south, emerging like a ghostly giant lumbering on to the island, in the half-light. As she reached the narrow footpaths, she abandoned her bicycle by a 'Climbers' signpost pointing to the cliffs and walked. She could smell the sea already.

Up ahead was a crystal clear rainbow, reaching from the west of the island into the sea. Miranda paused and gasped. It was so sharply drawn, she could see the different colours clearly; blue, purple, indigo and violet, glittering in the sky and melting into the sea. A low rumble of thunder rolled across the sky, and the strange light flickered as the sun rolled from east to west, from sunrise to sunset. Miranda stopped and squinted.

'For crying out loud,' said Miranda. 'I might have guessed you would be hanging about. You're like the gnome of doom!'

'Ben and I rescued you yesterday, remember?' said Isabel.

'Oh, shut up. I was soaked when I got home. My mother was furious. I expect you both thought it was a great joke to dunk me in freezing cold sea water,' said Miranda. She was not in the mood for all this. She needed to be alone, to think about mermaids and the dreadful lure of the sea.

'That's not how it happened, Miranda. By the way, why didn't you get dressed before you left home?'

'I didn't have time. Anyway, I wasn't expecting to be waylaid by you. You're like some kind of weird highwayman. What's the matter with you? Why don't you get a life?'

Isabel felt a lurch of despair in her stomach, as the ground seemed to tip and roll beneath her. Over to the west, the sun was now setting and storm clouds rolled in over the sea. The time shift made her feel sick and off balance, as though she had suddenly travelled on a supersonic jet into another time zone.

'You look a bit foggy,' said Miranda. 'Like you're not really here. Like a ghost.'

Isabel looked down at her hands. They were ghostly and pale.

'I should see a doctor if I were you,' said Miranda. She put her hands on her hips and glared at Isabel. Her resemblance to Sally Lucke was astonishing. Isabel gnawed her nails, staring at Miranda.

Miranda glared back at Isabel, her fair hair frizzing out around her head in a wild halo, as if the electricity of the coming storm had charged her up.

Footsteps approached. Joseph Groves stalked up the path, hands in pockets, like a thundercloud, impatient and angry. 'There you are!'

He seized Miranda's arm and pulled her round to face him. 'Enough of your games. You have the coins with you, I take it.'

Miranda took a step back. 'How dare you!' she spluttered.

'The money is of no value to you. How would you spend it? A simple girl with no education. The islanders would burn you as a witch if you tried to spend that gold. You need me to manage this for you. Tell me how you came upon it. Was it washed ashore from the wreck of the Magdalene on Chesil Beach last autumn?' said Joseph.

Miranda was speechless. She stared at the man. He was tall with clear golden brown eyes. He smelled of tobacco and brandy. Miranda reached out to touch his velvet coat. Her fingers tingled. 'Ooh,' she said, wonderingly.

Joseph stared at her. 'Who are you?'

Miranda ran her hand down Joseph's sleeve.

'What do you know of my gold?' hissed Joseph angrily.

Miranda gazed at him, transfixed. 'What?'

'Gold, I want my gold.'

Miranda smiled vaguely. 'Gold, as in …?'

'She doesn't know anything about the gold,' said Isabel, stepping firmly between Joseph and Miranda. They were too close to the cliff edge here. The rocks fell sharply down to the sea far below.

Miranda ducked around her, and pushed her out of the way. 'Oh, you mean, the gold,' she said, smiling widely. 'I am sure we can discuss it.'

'Miranda, don't be stupid,' said Isabel.

Joseph batted Miranda's hand away and turned menacingly to Isabel, his eyes narrowed. 'She is not Sally. Do you take me for a fool? She is yet another useless wench with no sense to speak of!' he snarled.

'As for you! I know you! It is the spy that huddles by my window and lurks in the woods at night. We have unfinished business,' Joseph said. 'I never forget a face, that is certain. No doubt you remember the edge of my sword.'

'You're history,' said Isabel. 'Sally knows that you killed her father!'

Thunder rolled in across the sea. The sun had set and heavy clouds crept across the dull grey horizon.

A cool voice came from behind them. 'I do know of my father's death, Joseph Groves. I will be avenged for this! As for the gold, I found it, but not from any wreck, least none that we know of. I made a deal, and a poor one at that. I will not give you the gold for all you may demand it.' Sally looked calm and collected, her hair scraped back from her face in a knot. She looked like she had made a decision and would not turn back.

'Take back your engagement ring. It was shoddily given and ill meant and I have no need of such things. I have given the gold away. You will never have it.'

She threw the ring at Joseph. He looked at her for a long moment, his eyes narrowed, as if he hardly recognised the girl who stood in front of him. Then he looked from Sally to Miranda, obviously puzzled.

'Is this some enchantment? To force my hand into marriage?' he asked.

'Marry as you will. It is no matter to me. I am leaving the island tonight,' said Sally, decisively.

'How?' said Joseph, spitting his words. 'You have no means. You have nothing. No friends. No education. You are a poor, pitiful wretch. An ignorant village wench who should be grateful to me. I agreed to your deal and you will not back out. Wherever the gold is, it belongs to me now.'

'Marry as he will?' said Miranda, 'I take it he is single then.'

Sally laughed. 'You are welcome to him. He loves naught but sovereigns, and I was fool enough to seek them for him. He can be bought. What value is a man that can be bought for a handful of coins? He is a murderer and a scavenger.'

'More my mother's type, really,' said Miranda, nervously, backing away from them.

'Come with me,' she added under her breath to Isabel. Isabel shook her head. 'No, I can't. I have to stay.'

Miranda shrugged, as she headed for the footpath.

'No doubt she is another drunken relative of yours, Sally Lucke,' said Joseph.

Sally shook her head. 'I know not who she is, nor whence she came. Perhaps she is an angel, come to protect me.' Isabel smiled. She had never seen Miranda as an angel.

'I will not be lied to any longer. Give me the gold. For certain you are working with this fairy child to undo our deal,' Joseph threatened Sally.

'Leave her! It is not her concern. She has tried greatly to help me.'

Joseph unsheathed his sword and stepped towards Sally. 'No matter, you can join your father in the depths of Deadman's Bay.'

'I am not afraid of you,' said Sally coldly. 'You have harmed many and yet I know you will not harm me.'

Joseph snarled. He cast his sword away and seized Isabel. 'Then she will die for you.'

Low rumbles of thunder shook the ground as the storm closed in. Suddenly, there was the heavy beat of wings. 'I knew the dragon would be here!' gasped Isabel. 'At last!'

She pushed Joseph away as the great sea dragon flew overhead, passing over them like a huge, low-flying aircraft, with a roar. He flew so close that Isabel could see every mark on his gold and green belly. She gasped in wonder at the sheer power and size of the animal, turning to follow his flight as he soared in a circle over the cliffs and back towards them. Her ears boomed as his wings beat the air.

'A dragon!' breathed Sally. 'This is a judgement on you, Joseph. The child has called the dragon to punish you. She knows that you killed my father. Murderer! I tell you, tonight all that you treasure burns! I once was a simple girl who dreamed of being wed to you. No longer. Now the dragon will take you!'

Joseph pushed Sally away, his eyes fixed on the dragon, not looking, not seeing, as Sally teetered on the edge of the cliff, and fell backwards, her arms outstretched. Joseph stared wide-eyed and motionless after her. 'No!' cried Isabel. 'This can't happen!'

Isabel turned, stretched her arms out in front of her, and jumped, pushing herself as far from the edge of the cliff as she could, diving headlong into thin air.

As she fell, there was suddenly silence, as though for one last moment Isabel was finally connecting past and present, healing the rift in time that had brought her so far into the past, in search of a dragon.

She glimpsed holes in the cliff where the puffins lived, the tufts of grass, each individual spike perfect and glistening. She thought how odd it was, to be falling from a cliff such a long time before she was even born. She spun in slow motion down and down. As she fell, she saw the sea dragon swoop beside her, and dive below the waves. In the last second, she knew that she was not afraid.

Isabel hit the water with a bang that blasted the air from her lungs.

CHAPTER SEVENTEEN

4 JANUARY 2011

MRS GROVES CONFESSES

Mrs Greychurch and Mrs Groves sat quietly in the living room of the farmhouse. The huge grandfather clock ticked loudly in the corner. Other than this, there was a heavy silence in the room for a long time, broken only by the gentle snoring of Gregor on Mrs Greychurch's feet.

'Why didn't you tell me about the sea dragon?' she asked.

Mrs Groves continued to look at her hands. She had struggled to explain about the dragon. It had been her secret for so long that the animal had become part of her normal routine. Feed Gregor, settle the horses, sweep out the dragon. It was part of her day-to-day life.

'It's just an animal. Something to be cared for and left in peace. Like my old horses. Surely you can understand that I had to keep the whole thing quiet,' said Mrs Groves. 'Think of the fuss if the newspapers got hold of the story.'

Mrs Greychurch pictured herself on the front page of the *Dorset Echo*, her arm around a beaming dragon. 'You should still have told me, dear. A problem shared is a problem halved, after all.'

Mrs Groves was shocked. Her friend had never seemed

so understanding about dragons before.

'I think it's gone, in any case,' said Mrs Groves. 'I've checked for it several times since yesterday. It hasn't returned, not once as far as I can tell.'

'I think it was scared,' said Mrs Greychurch.

'Yes, you probably frightened it off, lashing out at it like that,' Mrs Groves replied, a little testily. 'I left you in charge of it, why didn't you keep a closer eye on the animal?'

'I think I nodded off,' said Mrs Greychurch, guiltily.

She dug out a card from her pocket. 'My cousin from Australia, Eric 'Koala' Greychurch, has written a note in his Christmas card. It arrived late, just this morning. He has traced a Dorset girl called Sally Lucke to the court of King James I, arriving in January 1616, and he is researching the subject for a book he plans to write. He wants to discuss the matter further with me.'

She showed the card to Mrs Groves who raised her eyebrows and smiled a little. 'So Sally Lucke left the island after all. How extraordinary to discover *that* after so many years. And all the stories about the dragon devouring the poor girl … all part of local folklore. Sally must have done well for herself if she made it to the royal court.'

'Apparently there is a wealth of information about her. She was a favourite of the king for many years,' said Mrs Greychurch.

The two women sat gazing at the card for a few minutes. Gregor awoke with a jump and shook out his fur, coating Mrs Greychurch with fluff. She rolled her eyes in exasperation. Outside the snowfall was slowing a little. Mrs Groves rose to her feet and looked out of the window, clearing the steamed-up pane with her sleeve. She could hear muffled voices. Gregor bounced hopefully around her, expecting his walk.

'Fire! Where is Joseph? Lead the horses from the stable.'

'Let the farmhouse burn. He would cheat us out of a few coins. Let it burn!'

Mrs Groves and Mrs Greychurch looked at the fire burning low in the grate. 'Is there anyone outside?' asked Mrs Greychurch.

'Not a soul,' replied Mrs Groves.

'I thought I heard something. This is a funny old building,' said Mrs Greychurch.

'Gregor needs his walk. Let's … No, Gregor, get down. Mind the vase! Oh no.' There was a loud smash as the glass vase broke into tiny pieces. Gregor's tail continued to swish. He was used to breaking things.

'I'll fetch his lead,' said Mrs Greychurch in a resigned voice.

Joseph threw open the door of the cottage. Cold air surged in with him and the fire in the hearth flickered and nearly died. His coat was soaked and tattered and black shadows circled his eyes.

'Did Sally leave coins with you for safekeeping? The sum was promised to me, for we were engaged,' he demanded.

Agnes leaped to her feet. 'Do not menace me, Joseph Groves. I am not afraid of you. The men still scour the island for Sally, but you are here searching for gold. That tells me much! What happened this evening? I know well Sally planned to return your ring,' said Agnes.

'That is not your business. If you have the gold, I will take it, by force if necessary. My men protect your interests, you would burn as a witch were it not for me. You would do well to hand the coins over now.'

'I will teach you a lesson, Joseph Groves. It is in my power. If you have anything to do with Sally's disappearance, terrible things will befall you.'

There were voices outside, men shouted in the distance. 'We have her ring! It lay by the cliffs.'

'The sea dragon was sighted! Old John Muddle saw it fly.

An omen! Sally is lost!' The voices carried to them.

'Keep your curses, Agnes, you do not scare me …' Joseph was again interrupted.

'The Groves Farm is on fire! There are flames yonder! Where is Joseph? This is a cursed night.'

Agnes laughed. 'This is not my doing. It is God's hand. Villains easily find their own undoing! I do not need to help. Be assured, Joseph, Sally left me nothing of value, nothing but trouble.'

Joseph slammed the door behind him.

Agnes sat heavily at the kitchen table, her head in her hands. 'Sally, I pray you live still. You have left me with fine matters to resolve.'

Agnes turned the letter from Sally over in her hands and read aloud,

"Cousine, feare not for me. I have made a decisione of much consequence and Mother must fende for Herself. Tis not my job to kepe her now Father is gon, God only knows where he rests, God blesse his soul. I have made poore choices of late and cannot remain on the islande. Sadly, I must flee tonighte. I will forward to you Monies to care for my Familie and to improve matters for Yourselfe. Beware Joseph Groves for he intendes Harme. Yet He will know the Error of this shortly when I have Returned his Precious Ring."

'You always had high dreams, Sally' she sighed. 'Now I fear you have paid a terrible price for them. I hoped that the child Isabel would help you. Perhaps both of you are gone, lost forever.'

CHAPTER NINETEEN

4 JANUARY 2011

GREGOR ATTACKS

Mrs Greychurch and Mrs Groves walked in friendly silence, with Gregor on a short lead. He enjoyed walks, by and large, but had to be kept away from cars, bicycles, strangers, fences, hedgehogs, certain other dogs, snails and anything large that moved.

'He's very nervous of horses at the moment,' said Mrs Groves.

'But you run a stables!' said Mrs Greychurch, exasperated. 'Surely it is time you took Gregor back to dog training classes.'

'He has been banned from all the classes on the island,' said Mrs Groves. 'Honestly, they expect dogs to behave well the moment they walk into a class. Anyway, groups of dogs over-excite him, and he bites dog owners if they get too close to him. One stupid woman patted him!'

'How is her finger?'

'I think the bandages are off. We took her some flowers,' said Mrs Groves.

Gregor's eyes swivelled from side to side, looking for things waiting to attack him. There was a clunk. 'Gregor, mind the lamp post. Look where you're going, you silly dog.' He shook his head dizzily and sat down.

'We are never going to get anywhere at this rate,' said Mrs Greychurch impatiently.

'He'll be all right in a minute. Gregor gets tense if he's rushed on a walk.'

It was still early morning, very cold, and a light sea mist hid the sea below them at the foot of the cliffs, although they could hear the hiss of waves against the rocks. Perhaps the sea dragon was flying nearby. Mrs Groves found it comforting that her friend knew about the dragon at last. It felt like a weight had lifted from her shoulders.

Strangely, Miranda had cycled straight past them earlier. Gregor had lunged into the wheels barking furiously and Miranda had called the dog a stupid furball, which both Mrs Groves and Mrs Greychurch pretended not to hear.

'Nice to see her out and about so early, getting fresh air,' reflected Mrs Greychurch.

'Odd about the nightdress, though,' said Mrs Groves.

'Yes, but of course she did have her coat on as well.'

Mrs Groves looked sideways at her friend.

'Miranda wants to come back home. I must say I've missed her terribly. Things at boarding school are not all that she had hoped for.'

'Spoilt minx', thought Mrs Groves.

'So all's well that ends well, I think,' said Mrs Greychurch.

Up ahead they could hear shouting, muffled by the mist. There was a distant splash. Mrs Groves tentatively peered over the cliffs but there was nothing but white swirling fog. 'How odd. Is it just me or is it suddenly getting much colder? And that wind is blowing up.' She pulled her hat down firmly over her ears.

'Yes. It is freezing,' agreed her friend.

From the mist, a setting sun was emerging, and dark hail clouds edged across the sky. Gregor growled. The fur along his back stood up on end. There was a flash of lightning.

'Oh no. He's getting agitated. All we need now to completely set him off is a horse!' said Mrs Groves, looking around her anxiously.

The large black horse was tethered to a fence. Despite the cold, its shanks gleamed with sweat as though it had been ridden hard along the cliffs. It rolled its eyes, neighing and edging sideways when it saw them.

Gregor went berserk.

'I've got him! Down, Gregor. Sit! Sit!' shouted Mrs Groves frantically. Gregor was hysterical, his bark turning into a high-pitched yodel.

'Hold him down. I'll stand in front of the horse. He might forget it's there.'

It started to hail, a heavy drenching downpour that left them all soaked in seconds. They did not notice the tall, dark figure stalking towards them.

'You would attack my horse?' he accused.

The two women looked him up and down – from his tarnished riding boots to his burgundy coloured velvet coat, and his handsome but furious face. 'Goodness me,' said Mrs Greychurch to Mrs Groves. 'It's Captain Jack Sparrow from *Pirates of the Caribbean*.' She smoothed her hair and rearranged her dress.

'Witches! You spy on me, you plan to destroy me! You send dragons!' he roared. He grabbed Mrs Greychurch, as if he meant to throw her over the cliff. 'You will not bear witness against me, witch. None will believe an old crone. Leastways, not a dead one!'

Mrs Groves released Gregor, who flew at the man like a baying wolf, knocking him flat and sinking his teeth into his leg.

'Old crone!' said Mrs Greychurch, horrified.

'I think we'd better nip down here,' said Mrs Groves, pulling her astounded friend behind her. 'A short-cut across the field. I don't like the look of him.'

'What about Gregor?'

'He's fine, he'll catch us up. He'll distract the man while we get away,' said Mrs Groves breathlessly, looking over her shoulder.

'I know him from somewhere,' said Mrs Greychurch, also out of breath.

'Yes, although I can't quite remember where,' said Mrs Groves.

Gregor bounded up behind them, a piece of cloth hanging from his mouth, looking pleased with himself.

'Good boy, heel,' said Mrs Groves, clipping on his lead. 'See, he doesn't need training. He came to heel beautifully. Anyway, I think we should head home for a cup of tea.'

Gregor led the way with a triumphant gleam in his eye. He kept the piece of clothing clenched between his teeth and tucked it in his dog bed as a trophy when he got home.

CHAPTER TWENTY

4 JANUARY 1616

SALLY DISAPPEARS

Isabel plunged into the dark green sea, deeper and deeper. She saw the tips of fingers below her, disappearing into the endless depths, and grasped them tightly. They were freezing cold, colder even than the sea. Isabel kicked for the surface, pulling Sally Lucke behind her.

A shoal of tiny silver fish swam past. Isabel felt her legs growing weaker as the intense cold numbed every muscle in her body. From the corner of her eye, she saw the sea dragon swim past them, glimpsing the flickering lights of his scales.

Isabel saw the last breath leaving her body, a trail of bubbles rushing away from her. Now she had no sense of above or below. There was no light or dark, beginning or end, just infinite deep green. Tiny stars appeared in front of her eyes. Her cold fingers held on to the icy hand in her grasp.

Suddenly the dragon caught them, lifting them in a terrifying rush towards the surface of the sea. Isabel gasped for air, clasping the slippery scales of the sea dragon as it surfed through the icy waves and left them there, flying free of the water in one powerful movement.

Sally coughed and spluttered, opening her eyes. 'Look,' she said, 'Over there. My boat. It is laden. My brother waits for me there.'

A small blue fishing boat bobbed at the foot of the cliffs. Isabel swam beside Sally, with painful aching arms.

As they neared the boat, Sally pulled Isabel to her and looked at her intently. Seawater dripped down her face, still blue with cold. Through chattering teeth she said, 'Tell Agnes I am free at last. All has not gone as I intended, yet all will be well. I will make amends where needed. I will start my life anew. The islanders will not laugh at poor Sally any longer, to them I am dead and gone. I leave the island tonight. If I ever return, it will not be as Sally Lucke.'

Shivering violently, Sally hauled herself on to the small boat, taking a rug from her brother and throwing it around her shoulders.

Isabel turned and swam heavily for the shore, climbing out of the sea on to slippery Blacknor Rock, where she lay, her face against the cold smooth stone.

'Sso,' hissed the mermaid. 'You chosse to ignore my requesst.'

Close to, the mermaid's skin was white and cold, like a statue, her stare hard and glassy. She could be thousands of years old, as ancient as a piece of marble from the island of Atlantis, as ancient and exotic as the sea dragon.

'You are sso pleased to be alive. Yet you are far from home. Hundredss of yearss, in fact. How will you return? What if you can't? What if you are trapped here forever?' said the mermaid, with a sinister smile.

Isabel gasped for breath. Rain and hail poured from black skies lit by sharp flickers of lightning. The mermaid's eyes glittered.

'You think you know magic, like Agness.'

Isabel shook her head. The sharp hail stung her skin, as if needles bombarded her from the skies.

'We will have a deal, Issabel Maydew. I will return you to your time if you send me the child Miranda. She iss mine, by right, for you and Ssally have betrayed me.'

'No,' said Isabel, staggering to her feet. 'You ...' she pointed at the mermaid, as she tried to stand on the slippery rock, '... you have no power over me. I came here to find the dragon, the sea dragon. I will find my own way home.'

Exhausted, Isabel stumbled away from the mermaid, the hail pouring in lines in front of her, so that she could barely see. She jumped from Blacknor Rock to the other stones that jutted from the sea. The tide was surging in now, and the Rock was disappearing under waves. The winds howled in from the west. Thunder roared around her. She took the cliff steps, slipping and sliding, the hail lying like white crystals on the rock. Isabel felt her way with her hands, taking one step at a time. Finally Agnes's cottage loomed ahead of her, hardly more than a shadow in the storm.

She collapsed under the porch, her head resting against the oak door. Exhausted, she fell into a dreamless sleep. The rain drummed on the roof and the storm vented its fury on the island.

Voices murmured around her. 'Should we waken her?' said Rian, Agnes's daughter.

As her eyes opened, Agnes leaned over her. 'What became of you? You are soaked! Fancy being out in such a storm!'

Isabel blinked at her.

'A terrible hailstorm! Never have we seen such a storm on the island. Many cottages have been blown to shreds. Some saw the sea dragon swooping across the island. And Sally Lucke is lost. They say the dragon took her. Did you see anything?' said Agnes.

'The dragon didn't harm her. Joseph ...,' croaked Isabel.

'Catastrophe befell him also this very night. A fire sweeps through the farmhouse. His men left the search for Sally and tried to stop the flames but, even in this storm, it is burning to the ground. It is a judgement on him, I am sure.'

Agnes helped Isabel to her feet and took her to the fireplace, where a log fire roared. Her daughter Rian sat on a kitchen chair looking at Isabel with large, curious grey eyes.

'The farmhouse was robbed, all the Groves' wealth taken, Joseph's gold gone. Mind, he dare not admit how much, for the Customs officers will ask too many questions. So will his own men, who he cheated at every turn. Whoever stole from him, they picked a good time, all the people of the isle distracted by the storm and the dragon. Joseph is in a terrible fury, riding around in search of those who betrayed him. No one is talking.'

Agnes raised her eyebrows at Isabel. 'Smugglers have many friends when they have goods to share. A different story when they have nothing.'

Isabel looked thoughtfully at Agnes. Sally had won in the end. Isabel remembered the small boat waiting for Sally at the foot of the cliffs. No doubt it had been loaded up with Joseph's gold, as well as her own. Sally had fled the island, leaving fire and mayhem behind her. What would she do with all that gold? Isabel could not help smiling as she thought about it.

Agnes watched Isabel with narrowed eyes. 'So you flit to and fro at will,' she said at last. 'It's a dangerous game, child. Sally has left me with awkward matters to resolve. I can only pray she is alive. She has returned my book, with a letter. Do you know what she intends to do?' Agnes held the gleaming *Monsteres of the Air and Sea* in her hands.

'Sally took a boat to the mainland ...' said Isabel.

'Well, well,' said Agnes. 'Who would have thought? Sally Lucke has made a fool of Joseph Groves. I have many questions for you, Isabel Maydew, as I guess we should call you. You are a time traveller, no less, from a world that is yet to come.'

Isabel rose to her feet and stretched.

'Mother, let her go, it is not the time to ask questions, it is better not to know what the future holds,' said Rian in her quiet voice.

Already, the fragile first light of a winter dawn crept through the window, the storm a distant bank of purple clouds across the horizon. Agnes took Isabel's hand in hers and looked into her eyes. Isabel was almost as tall as Agnes, their eyes virtually level.

'Perhaps better for me to ask the time traveller, have your questions been answered, Isabel? It takes a strong desire to take a person across time. It is powerful magic. Did you find what you were looking for?'

Isabel looked around the tiny cottage, with its haphazard stone floors, simple wooden table and crooked chairs. She looked at the serious faces of Agnes and her daughter. 'I came here looking for a sea dragon,' she said, 'and for a witch – as a matter of fact, the Maydew witch.'

'So they call me,' Agnes laughed.

'Anyway,' continued Isabel. 'I found something much better, something really special. I found real people, living their lives, I have learned a lot, and I know that the Maydew witch is doing her best for the people on the island. The sea dragon is amazing too, but I think he just wants to be left alone. I've solved the mystery of Sally's disappearance, she is safe and well, and the dragon helped her. This isn't a tragic night for her any more. Now I have to go home.'

Agnes nodded and hugged her. 'It's time for you to go home, then. Give my good wishes to your family, to the Maydews of the future. I will leave the book for you. It is very precious, the only one of its kind. I will give it to Rian to pass on to her daughter, and she will pass it to her daughter too, until one day it reaches you.'

Isabel smiled. 'I always knew that the book was meant to be mine!'

'Tell your family about the Maydew witch and Sally Lucke, so that our names live and breathe, not just as words on a page in a book. Then, truly, we shall live forever. Who can ask for more than that?'

Agnes closed the door behind her and Isabel walked alone into the garden, the air fresh and bright after the storm. She could hear an early skylark high above, celebrating the start of a new day. Tiny sprigs of green showed through the cold ground, the first glimpse of the hardy snowdrops.

The sea dragon was waiting for her, as she had hoped and dreamed for such a long time. Steam rose from his long shiny green nose and he blinked with large sad yellow eyes at her. In the clear morning light, she could see the vivid colour of his scales, greens, golds and shimmering shades that ranged beyond the rainbow. She noticed how still and patient he was.

Isabel uncurled her hand to him. The dragon stooped, steam hissing from his nostrils, and looked carefully at her. Isabel patted his nose and backed away from him. He dipped his head as if he were asking her to come closer, and lowered one of his wings. Isabel softly rested her hands on his spiky back and jumped up, as if she were climbing on to Isaac. She clung on to the spikes. The dragon turned his head to look at her with one yellow eye, then he flapped his wings with a powerful whoomph and lifted easily into the sky.

Isabel felt her stomach lurch as they shot straight up, higher and higher over the island, until Agnes's cottage was just a small dot. The dragon tipped to the left as he turned steadily. The wind roared through Isabel's ears. She was laughing and crying at the same time. It was the most exciting flight ever. Far below, she could see the West Cliff. The dragon turned again, heading north. He followed the line of Chesil Beach, heading towards the mists of Moonfleet, surging low over the waves that crashed against the pebbles, until Isabel could feel the sting of salty spray against her face, then up again and around the lagoon and back towards Portland.

Beside them, a new rainbow tracked their journey, running like a river of colour, following them with red, orange, green and purple. Silver lightning zigzagged from the sky into the sea below, and thunder roared around the island.

They approached the island again from the west. Agnes's

cottage had gone and in its place were the familiar blocks of flats and small painted houses of 2011. As they landed gently on the grassy field beside the cliffs, where they had started their journey, Isabel tumbled to the ground and sat gazing up at the sea dragon. He tipped his head at her, as if he found her curious, a puzzle, then he took off again. He soared low over Isabel. Then, with a final flap of his wings, he vanished. Isabel knew she would never see him again.

So many things had happened to Isabel since she left home, but in reality she had been away for just an hour or two. The frost under her feet crackled as she walked home to Suzie and her mother, following the familiar path. The snow glistened around her and the warm green of the grass shone through the melting ice. The air smelled different, cool and clear.

Isabel opened the garden gate and was greeted by a soft 'Baa'. A large sheep draped in a pink fleecy blanket gazed peacefully at her. Beside him, Suzie knelt in her pyjamas, a blissful smile on her face, her cheeks rosy with excitement. 'I woke up and you were gone, so I climbed out the window and got a sheep!'

Ben blinked blearily up at her from beside Suzie. He was sitting on an upside down wheelbarrow in his dressing gown and wellington boots. 'I couldn't stop her! She woke me up! She made me help her!'

Isabel shrugged. 'I suppose it could be worse.'

CHAPTER TWENTY ONE

5 JANUARY 2011

BACK HOME

Miranda and the mermaid perched on a rock by the sea near the Bill. The red and white lighthouse overlooked them, and the sea churned nearby, where the different currents met in the Portland 'race'. As the winter sun warmed the water, fragments of melting ice floated past them, like tiny icebergs. From time to time, dolphins leaped in the water, making their way south.

The mermaid looked bored. She rested her chin in her hands and her eyes were glazed. Miranda had been talking for half an hour, non-stop, about herself.

'... So I said, 'Mother, you look like an idiot in that orange t-shirt with *I Love Dragons* on it', but she said, 'Well, what do you young people know about fashion?' and I said, 'You can't go out looking like that! My friends might see you ...'

The mermaid yawned and interrupted, 'Ssisster, forever iss a long time.'

'What's that got to do with it?'

'Everything,' sighed the mermaid.

Miranda and the mermaid looked at one another. Finally the mermaid smiled, showing her sharp pointy teeth. She scooped her long waving hair over her shoulder.

'Daughter of Ssally, we will meet another day, another time. I am ssure your mother needss you more than we do.'

'She may need some help with her clothes, I haven't even told you what she was wearing with the t-shirt! It was hideous!' said Miranda, uncertainly.

'I inssist,' said the mermaid. 'You musst sstay here.'

'Whatever,' said Miranda, a bit miffed, and she started walking home.

What the Historians Say

From *The Court of the Stuart Kings*
by Eric Koala Greychurch,
published 2011

'Sally Anne Lucke arrived in the Court of King James I in 1616 on the arm of Knight of the Realm Sir Archie Longridge of Dorset. With a large personal fortune, she was considered to be the most dazzling woman in the country, regarded with envy by the women of the Court. It was never clear where she had come from, but she sometimes referred to the great country estates of her home in the south of England. She never married, but remained a regular at Court, her wit, charm and style always the toast of the town. The King plainly adored her.'

From *Sisters of the Land, a History of Women in Dorset*
by Rowena Groves, member of the Women's Suffrage Movement and early feminist,
first published 1908

'Agnes Maydew, widow, was well known for her work in the parish. Her only daughter Rian married Robert Groves, younger brother of Joseph Groves, a marriage that produced one child, Estelle Groves.

The Maydew family provide an excellent example of the strong role of women in rural society. Both Agnes and Rian Maydew played a vital role in their communities, in work such as providing herbal remedies, spinning and assisting the sick. Agnes also took in the Lucke children, a poor local family, and raised them as her own. The two eldest Lucke boys, Jacob and Richard, developed a successful quarrying business on the island and brought prosperity and respectability to the family in the mid 1600s. Their descendants continue to live on the island today.'

From *A History of Building in South Dorset*
by Robin Lucke, stonemason,
published 1934

'The Groves family suffered a major setback in January 1616. There was the inexplicable loss of the family fortune and the devastation of the farmhouse in a fire, reputedly set by local men who had been underpaid by Joseph Groves, although it was also rumoured that a betrayed love interest was responsible. Some local accounts also refer to a link with smuggling.

Joseph Groves received a large endowment of gold in 1616, from a London heiress, which enabled him to rebuild the farmhouse and restore the farm on a far more prosperous level. A study of the east portion of the farmhouse clearly indicates that a dramatic fire took place here. The identity of the heiress was not recorded, although farm records show that a 'grand lady' visited the farm many times over the years, and enjoyed a close friendship with Joseph Groves.

The farm was later inherited by Robert Groves, who lived there with his wife Rian Maydew and child Estelle.

WHAT THE NEWSPAPERS SAY

The *Dorset Echo*, 28 October 2009

It's a Monster!
The world's most ferocious predator – found in Dorset

'A fossilized skull of one of the largest predators ever known has been discovered on the Dorset coast. The skull of a pliosaur, a giant marine reptile that roamed the depths of the ocean around 150 million years ago, has been unveiled after it was unearthed by a fossil collector near Weymouth …

… The skull, which will eventually go on display at the Dorset County Museum, is over two metres long and it is believed the creature it came from could have measured up to 16m in length.

Pliosaur palaeontologist Richard Forrest said: "It is an extraordinary find. There are probably half a dozen specimens of this size in the world and this is the biggest complete pliosaur skull from anywhere in the world. It's not just of national importance, it's of international importance. It's going to tell us an awful lot about the biology of pliosaurs".

Reprinted by kind permission of the Dorset Echo

ABOUT THE AUTHOR

Carol lives on the island of Portland with her three children. She studied English Literature and History, and started writing *The Portland Chronicles* after walking around the island, inspired by the spirit of the place, its mystery and magic. Also, it was too windy and rainy to do anything else, and the children had colds. Carol has worked extensively with young people as an adviser. In her free time, she looks for sea dragons, mermaids and fairies.

About the Illustrator

Domini Deane is a self-taught artist, who has been creating magical worlds and creatures since she could pick up a crayon. Born in the Rocky Mountains of Colorado, she now lives and works in Dorset, England. Her favourite medium is watercolour with a pinch of fairy dust, and her greatest inspiration is a blank piece of paper.

For more information, please visit:
www.dominideane.com

ABOUT ROVING PRESS

Roving Press is a small publishing company in rural Dorset, near Dorchester. We love producing unusual, distinctive books, and it's been great fun putting together this one. Have a look at our website (**www.rovingpress.co.uk**) – it tells you about our books and authors, including Carol and what she's doing next.

If you would like a special signed copy or want to know when other *Portland Chronicles* become available give Julie or Tim a call. Happy reading!

OTHER ROVING PRESS TITLES

The Spirit of Portland: Revelations of a Sacred Isle
by Gary Biltcliffe

Roaring Dorset! Encounters with Big Cats
by Merrily Harpur

A Slice of Apple Pie: Your One-Stop Guide to Living in America
by Julie Musk

Lesser Known Swanage
by Julie Musk

Discover Old Swanage
by David Haysom